THE
GOOD
BEAR

THE GOOD BEAR

SARAH LEAN

illustrated by Fiona Woodcock

SIMON & SCHUSTER

First published in Great Britain in 2020 by Simon & Schuster UK Ltd

Text copyright © 2020 Sarah Lean
Illustrations copyright © 2020 Fiona Woodcock

1 3 5 7 9 10 8 6 4 2

Simon & Schuster UK Ltd
1st Floor, 222 Gray's Inn Road
London WC1X 8HB

www.simonandschuster.co.uk
www.simonandschuster.com.au
www.simonandschuster.co.in

Simon & Schuster Australia, Sydney
Simon & Schuster India, New Delhi

A CIP catalogue record for this book is available from the British Library.

HB ISBN 978-1-4711-9467-2
eBook ISBN 978-1-4711-9466-5
eAudio ISBN 978-1-4711-9637-9

Printed and bound by CPI Group (UK) Ltd, Croydon, CR0 4YY

MIX
Paper from
responsible sources
FSC® C020471

For Mum, thank you

CHAPTER ONE

Every year on Christmas Eve, Thea Whittington tells a story. It's about something that happened to her when she was a girl, more than thirty years ago.

Now, Thea is sitting on the sofa with a blanket peeled back while she waits for her daughter, Ursula, who is upstairs changing into her pyjamas.

It's dark outside and the sitting room smells of the sprigs of holly, twigs and pine cones tied with ribbons they collected that morning. There's a blueberry pie in the oven, and there's a Christmas tree, decorated except for the star, which lies against the crêpe-paper-wrapped bucket of sand at the foot of the tree. Across the room Thea's world-worn boots lie on the doormat. She holds a photograph; its colours have dimmed and the edges of the paper are soft. There are two figures in the picture; one of them is a man wearing a blue coat who is Thea's father, and the other is a brown bear. The bear has one great paw raised. Thea smiles at them, as if they can see her. She sets the photo aside as Ursula comes bounding down the stairs and jumps on the sofa.

They snuggle under the blanket with their mugs of hot chocolate and marshmallows. They blow and sip and bathe in the warmth and the glow of the little golden lights on the tree.

Hot drinks finished, they gather the blanket closer around them, tucking it in at the sides. Thea takes a corner of the photograph and holds it between them and they lean against each other for a full minute or two, taking in the image.

'I'm ready,' Ursula says.

'Where shall I start?' Thea asks, as she does every year on Christmas Eve.

'Start with the letter you wrote to Henry just before your twelfth birthday.'

'I'll start with the letter then.'

CHAPTER TWO

I didn't tell my mum about the letter at first. I didn't think she'd agree . . . but we'll come to that. About two weeks before my twelfth birthday, which was on the 11th December 1978, I wrote to my father, Henry, asking him if he would buy me a typewriter as a present. He and my mum had divorced when I was four and visits from him were irregular. Communication had all but stopped since he'd been living and working in Norway for the past few years. I had begun to think of him as Henry, the man who used to be my dad. It armoured me against the fact he had drifted away from my life, but at that time also had the effect of making me feel the distance between us and want to pull him back. I was worried he was missing not only that I had grown but also hearing about what was growing inside my heart. I aspired to be a writer, more than anything else in the world, and I especially wanted him to know about that.

Around that time, Mum was occasionally bringing home a typewriter from her office to do some typing in the evenings to earn extra money. To me, there was something special about watching her sitting with her elbows tucked in, head slightly to one side, eyes on the notes she'd been given. It was magic the way she transferred those handwritten words, so quickly, from her eyes through her fingers and then to the typewriter keys to form beautifully organized sentences on paper. I wanted something of what I saw, and yet much more, because I wanted it to be *my* words and *my* stories appearing like that. I told her I wanted to learn to type too.

Mum began to teach me to touch type. It meant resting my fingers on the middle line of keys, and then she would cover my hands with a tea towel so that I had to remember where the letters were. My fingers were learning to feel and know where to reach, as if my eyes were then free to turn inside me, and to somehow view, unhindered, the stories that would flow to the tips of my fingers. It was a wonderful feeling; a sense of knowing that I had something creative in me and it was my responsibility to find a way of letting it out.

With the urge in me so strong, I thought I must have a typewriter of my own. And to my mind, being a writer would also encourage Henry to want to be in my life so that he could share this part of me that I thought was worth sharing.

My handwriting was terribly time-consuming,

and a little flamboyant if anything, with lots of loopy tails and flourishes on the long and high letters. It had caused Mum and my teachers some concern as I took so long to finish things at school and often had to stay behind in break time to catch up. But I was much more interested in the words themselves and what they could do. I wrote the letter to Henry by hand because I thought it was also important that he should see how much of a hindrance my handwriting was to me. I crossed out the sentiments I felt were somehow weak. I screwed the paper up many times, started again and again, worrying over whether I had said enough or if Henry would be able to tell how much it all meant to me. Using the most dazzling descriptions, even though I barely understood them, and with the most compelling persuasion I could muster, the letter with my birthday present wish for a typewriter slowly got written, loopy tails and all. I copied Henry's address from a scrappy piece of paper tucked inside our address book and searched the drawers of the sideboard for a loose stamp. I sneaked out while Mum was hand-washing delicates at the kitchen sink and ran to the corner of our road.

I turned the envelope over, checked the seal and pressed my thumb over the stamp again. Then I dropped it in the post box before doubt got the better of me.

My heart fluttered with anticipation every time I thought of that letter getting closer and closer to him. The desire that was winging its way to him in its envelope was out of my hands now, and hopefully safely in his.

For my birthday Mum bought me a satchel. It was brown leather with two buckles and a long strap, and expanded in the middle. I tried it out, wearing it across my chest, deeming it my version of a writer's briefcase, in preparation and rehearsal for what I wanted to be.

No present had arrived from Henry though.

All he sent was a card.

On seeing me so miserable, I told Mum about the letter. She winced, and not just a little, when I admitted what I'd asked Henry for. She thought I shouldn't have handed over to Henry such a big wish as this one. I explained to her that my letter and request were my way of trying to draw us closer together. I was sure he'd understand from my words how important it was for me because of his own passion for working with wood.

Despite Mum's reservations, somewhere between my disappointing birthday and some phone calls she made, it was decided I should spend Christmas with Henry and his new family. It wasn't what I'd imagined would happen. I'd hoped for the gift, and perhaps a card with a letter inside, and meaningful words.

'But that means *we* won't spend Christmas together,' I told Mum. The thought of missing out on that precious time with traditions we had made our own was enough to make me refuse. It was only for this one Christmas, Mum assured me, a little more than one week away from each other. And although we would miss each other terribly, she thought I should go.

'Henry told me he does have a birthday present for you,' she said, wincing again.

'He does?' I took her reaction to mean that she knew what gift awaited me in Norway but didn't want to spoil the surprise.

I took myself off to my room and stretched out the pleated middle of my satchel. There was enough room for a small, portable typewriter, one that might have been too heavy or too big to post from Norway.

My father had long been gone and I had in many ways accepted his absence as I loved the life I shared with Mum. Life had also added a new family to Henry over in Norway, and although I felt slightly envious over the fact they had him in their daily life, I gave them little other thought. As far as I was concerned, I was on my way to becoming a writer, which happened to involve an important journey to see my father first and collect the typewriter.

CHAPTER THREE

Eight days after my birthday, Mum took me to catch a plane to Norway. As we said goodbye, I told her to look under my bed on Christmas Eve.

Mum said however much she would miss me that I should spend my time away working out what I wanted most, with Henry, with my writing, and there was no need to phone her unless there was an emergency.

'I know you can do this all by yourself, Thea.'

'Can I call you just to say hello?' I was worried about being so far from home and Mum, and also about seeing Henry again after so long.

'Hello is very expensive from Norway,' she said, kissing me. 'All will be well, because of that good brave heart of yours.'

I sat by myself on the plane with my satchel buckled into the seat with me. While I was in Norway, I intended to write about my holiday on my new typewriter. I'd type it up and bring it back for Mum so that my story about the reunion with my father would fill in for the time we'd have been apart.

Soon the concerns of leaving Mum behind turned to thoughts of who I was going to meet. My memories of Henry from when he lived with Mum and me had merged with the character of a woodsman from a fairy tale; a slightly untamed man who'd leave us for the forest and often not come back at dinner time. He was a skilled craftsman and made furniture and other objects from wood. He would be gone for hours searching for fallen trees to work with, including those sacred family Sunday afternoons when he should have been with us. At times he'd been sought out for his skill as a carpenter, taking commissions to build unique pieces of furniture, but it had consumed him entirely and left little room for us or any sense of family unit. In the end, Mum had given up trying to make him into something other than he was. I believed he must still love me and I had never asked anything of him until now. But I was feeling a little tested by the fact that he was living in Norway within another family, with three *other* children, none of whom were biologically his. I consoled myself with the one important inheritance from Henry that they would not have: I had a passion just like he did. I believed it was the connection that would prove our relationship to be stronger than the one they might have made.

At Oslo airport, an air stewardess accompanied me to the arrivals gate and asked, 'Thea, what does your father look like?'

'He has brown frizzy hair, like me. His name's Henry Whittington. He's this tall,' I told her, raising my arm to give him a height in the space beside me. 'Imagine a woodsman from a fairy tale who smells of sawdust. Oh, and his favourite colour is blue. He loves the colour blue.'

I wanted to tell the air stewardess that I was going to be a writer and that Henry might even greet me with the late birthday present I was expecting, but I think she was a little confused at my description. Perhaps she hadn't read any fairy tales. She squinted as she scanned the excitable crowd behind the barrier waiting to greet loved ones, probably wondering how she could identify a person who liked blue.

'There he is,' I said. He stood like a rugged Scots pine among a swathe of shivering birch trees. His beard and wild hair had grown like honeysuckle left to roam where it willed. He wore a blue knitted hat and a blue quilted coat, just as I'd imagined but hadn't quite been able to get across. Henry wasn't by himself though, nor was he carrying my belated present. His new partner and two of her children had come along.

I put my arms around Henry's waist and buried my face in the blue of his coat. He patted my back, letting go of me after two seconds. It's a secret habit of mine to count the seconds during the length of a hug or the linger of a kiss, although I try very hard not to do that any more. Henry's loose hug wasn't nearly long enough to mark the importance of us being apart for years and now together again.

Henry had a habit, which I'd quite forgotten, of starting sentences with a short low growl as if he needed those nearby to know that he was about to speak but that it pained him to be pleasant and chatty.

'Say hello to everyone,' Henry said, in his gruff, awkward way.

Everyone is a wonderful word, suggesting togetherness, but I didn't feel included. I was disappointed by his brisk welcome and felt as if I hadn't quite been invited in yet.

Henry's girlfriend was called Inge. She had rosy cheeks, burned by cold winds, and wore chunky knitted accessories with woolly tassels. The first thing she said was that they could all speak English very well and would for my benefit. Hess, her eldest son, was abroad, she told me, and wouldn't be home for Christmas. I would be sleeping in his room. She introduced me to her daughter and we exchanged reluctant hellos. Elissa was sixteen and looked as unwilling as I was to make a new relationship. And then there was Lars, with straw-yellow curls that looked as if a pile of tagliatelle had been dropped on his head. I think he was also twelve at the time. He feebly flapped his hand at me.

I had inherited my father's unruly hair and I pushed my way to stand next to him so that the others were all facing us. I hoped they could see that I was undoubtedly his, and they, with their blondness, were not. I had assumed he would be coming to collect me alone. I had imagined him mentioning my letter and asking me about my writing as we rekindled the bond between us on the journey to his house. Already I had taken exception to the new family and not having what I thought was my fair share of Henry: the biggest share.

There we were, gathered together yet standing apart. I had already decided how I felt about each of them on first appearances, but was completely unaware of what more I was about to encounter.

CHAPTER FOUR

Henry said, 'Let's get going,' preceded by another awkward growl.

I asked him if he'd received my letter. I probably should have been forewarned by the fact that he nodded and nodded, as if he'd been reminded of something that had slipped his mind.

'There's a present for you back at the house,' he said. I wondered if he too was hopeful of the present being the way of finding out more about me. I decided to put my faith in the gift. That's where we'd have to begin properly.

Henry loped ahead, pushing firmly against the revolving door at the exit from the airport. As the door turned me out too, I was shocked by the crystal-sharp cold that needled its way through my school coat. Mum and I had packed the warmest clothes I owned, but even if I had worn all my jumpers at once I wouldn't have been protected from the freezing temperatures of winter.

'There's no bad weather in Norway, only bad clothes,' Inge said to me. I clung to the collar of my jacket, pinning it around my neck, smarting at having my clothes disapproved of. Already I was wishing Henry could have come to Britain instead, where I would have had him to myself.

Inge drove. She had a camper van that rattled so loudly it was impossible to have a conversation or hear the radio, but it was probably just as well as everyone was avoiding making eye contact.

Instead, I stared through a hole I'd cleared in the steamed window. Outdoors at home, Christmas week was always grey and damp, the trees bare. Perhaps that's why I appreciated the warmth of our home, glowing and sparkling with decorations. But Norway truly was a wonderland wrapped in white.

It looked like Christmas itself, decorated with countless evergreen trees, sculpted with perfect snow like the picture on our festive biscuit tin.

Their house was at the edge of a small town, standing all by itself, the last one before the woods and the wilds. The walls were made of planks of wood, the bark still skinning them, with a wide overhanging roof. To the side were a single-storey workshop, a double garage and a log store. Snow had been cleared from the drive and away from the front of the house, piled on either side as high as my chest. I'd never seen so much snow, smooth and thick everywhere, topping the roof like Christmas-cake icing. We got out of the van and I followed them up the path lined with crisp white snow, under the porch with silvery icicles and into the house. It was such a disappointment. Inside there wasn't a hint of tinsel or decoration to give a clue as to the time of year. My heart sank that I was missing out on home, Mum, and our tree and the decorations we had collected and made over the years.

While I unpacked in Hess's room, I could hear everyone moving around downstairs, speaking Norwegian, which made me feel even more like an outsider. I heard the front door closing as someone went out, and panicked that Henry might have left me alone with them all. I jumped up and looked out of the window and saw Elissa in her yeti boots and knitted bobble cap trotting down the road as if she'd been waiting for the moment to escape. I sat back on the bed like a guest at a hotel with a knot tying in my stomach, scanning the trophies of small figures of boys playing ice hockey on an otherwise empty polished wooden desk, hoping Henry would come up by himself with my belated birthday present.

Inge called up the stairs in Norwegian and I heard Lars answer from outside in the hallway. There was a knock at the bedroom door and Lars swung it open wearing thick knitted slipper socks that had slouched down around his ankles.

'When are you coming down?' he said. He checked around the room to see if I had disturbed any of Hess's trophies.

'Would you tell *Henry* to come up?' I said. I made the point of not saying 'Dad'. I didn't want to accept that that was who he was to Lars.

'*Inge* said you have to come down to try on a coat,' he said, copying the way I had stressed Henry's name, and left the room. I had little intention of getting to know him but went downstairs anyway.

Their house smelled of woodsmoke. Knitted cushion covers and blankets in primary colours and geometric patterns softened most surfaces, fabric bags were stuffed with balls of wool beside easy chairs. The kitchen, dining room and sitting area were open plan, so there was nowhere to hide easily. Even worse was that the whole place showed no sign at all that Christmas was coming. Mum and I used to glitter-up our house. We were tinsel and fairy-light fanatics. We always put the decorations up the day before my birthday. That way, Christmas and my birthday seemed like one long celebration. I realize now that this was probably to make up for the fact that the other half of my parents showed little or no interest in either of those things. Perhaps Henry had found himself a family who cared as little as he did for celebratory events. Suddenly, I longed for home, for everything familiar. I couldn't bear the thought of spending Christmas here when I was not part of this family.

Henry was sitting by himself in a chair by the open fire. He was never very good at socializing but I resented the fact that having travelled so far to see him he didn't even try to make me feel welcome. Inge, however, was waiting for me with more suitable clothing for a Norwegian winter.

'This should do for you, Thea,' she said, holding a coat out for me to try. 'It gets so cold and you'll want to go out and explore, won't she, Lars?'

Lars jumped on the sofa with a small carved wooden plane, fell on his back and held the toy up, flying it around. He was too embarrassed to answer and I was too embarrassed to look at him. The thick padded coat was not to my taste and too big for me. I looked and felt absolutely swamped, and of all the awful colours a coat could be, it was, to my mind, the worst. Cowpat-brown.

'It's Elissa's old coat, but she won't mind,' Inge said. I imagined the conversation that she'd already had, and that even though Elissa might have been unwilling to offer me much, she was probably glad to let me have the awful coat.

I tried to be polite but it wasn't easy. I glanced towards Henry, but he busied himself with constructing a pyramid of logs to feed the fire. I think I said the coat was warm, or something like that, even though I felt and looked like a jacket potato. And as if that wasn't bad enough, Inge pulled a rabbit-fur hat with ear-flaps over my head, saying it was hers but I could keep it.

I was hot and bothered now. Nothing fitted properly. Neither the clothes nor the people. It could have been any day of the year, not a reunion with my father, not the special week before Christmas, not my belated birthday. Thankfully, the rectangular box on the table caught my eye.

I had to focus on the present instead. The typewriter was what I wanted and it would give me a good excuse to be by myself in my room and write. Of course, I was assuming Henry and I would spend some time together over the week, so I could show him my writing.

'Happy birthday,' Henry said, nudged by Inge, like a man thrown into a new part in a play with only seconds to learn his lines. He nodded towards the gift-wrapped box. 'It's from all of us.'

I tore the paper carefully. I had invested my whole heart in this moment and how wonderful I had imagined it would be, having rehearsed it in my mind time and time again. I wanted to savour every second and the significance of it to have a huge effect on Henry, as well as the others. I gushed and giggled before I'd even opened it, badly over-egging my sense of delight. I wanted to be sure that Henry would know how much it meant to me and that he was the one who had fulfilled my greatest wish.

I lifted the lid.

Inside the box was a pair of rubber boots.

CHAPTER FIVE

I could not believe my eyes. In fact, it was only my nose that seemed to be working as I registered the smell of new rubber. I moved one of the boots, lifting it up to see if a typewriter was underneath because I could not comprehend how Henry had got it so wrong.

The typewriter, the important birthday present, was also meant to be the key to pulling Henry back into my life, keeping contact with him in the best way I knew how – with written words. My vision had been of long, typed letters between us (they'd be long, I was sure, as I had so much to say), along with the stories I loved to write and wanted to share with him. I hoped for him to be proud that I had a passion like he did. How would *boots* help me to be a real writer?

'Now you have everything for going out in the snow,' Inge said. 'I think I guessed a good size? Try them and see.'

Henry hadn't even chosen the boots! For a second, I thought Henry must be about to produce *another* present. The typewriter. But he was already on his way outside, wearing his own coat and boots and carrying a steaming coffee cup. He said something to Inge in Norwegian, which he must have known I couldn't understand, and she replied, 'English, Henry'. I felt forgotten already, cast out from his new life altogether because he had to be reminded I spoke the language he was also born with.

'I'll be in the workshop,' he said now, to nobody

in particular. 'I need to get that sledge finished for the Brustad family before Christmas.' Henry left me then, with *his* other family. I felt as if I'd been dropped off at an after-school club that I hadn't signed up for.

Inge placed the boots on the floor and I had no choice but to step into them. She pressed at the empty space around my toes. The boots were also too big.

'Thick socks will help,' she said.

'I only have these kinds of socks,' I said, humiliation turning into sourness on my tongue because I didn't seem to fit in with anything at all.

'You can borrow some from Lars,' she said.

For me it was getting worse and worse. Lars was leaning over the back of the sofa, staring at me with what I thought might be pleasure, as if he knew that I'd been anticipating so much more and was pleased at me being put in my place. Inge asked him to go and find me some socks. He slumped his way upstairs, still holding the little wooden plane. And then I realized that the plane Lars was carrying had probably been made by Henry. I could not believe *my* father had shared his love of wood with somebody else's boy but couldn't recognize how much his own daughter wanted a typewriter.

'Okay, so it's all good?' Inge said.

As she stood there, waiting, I knew I was supposed to say thank you, but I couldn't say it. Not even to be polite. Inge looked uncomfortable because she probably wasn't sure what was wrong. At first, I doubted whether she'd seen the letter that I wrote to Henry, but then I wondered if she had and that she might not have cared what I'd asked for. In my growing state of dejection, I even imagined Inge had intended the boots to be some kind of message, warning me that I was no longer in my father's favour or special to him in any way now he had her children to care for. I felt completely alone. I wanted to cry but I wouldn't in front of her.

My feelings snowballed.

'You must be tired after travelling,' Inge said. She put on her own coat and boots and said she'd be out in the workshop too if I wanted to come and join them and see what Henry was making.

It's a dreadful thing to not say thank you. And refusing to be grateful does terrible things to you too, and as a consequence my heart became blackened like a chimney coated with soot. A dam of tears was about to break and I had to get away.

Lars came down the stairs. 'It's best to wear two pairs of socks,' he said. He was carrying the whole drawer of socks and pants that he'd brought from his chest of drawers. I expect he felt he couldn't possibly know which ones I would want.

I ran to the front door.

'Where are you going?' he said.

I had to stick my chin up so the tears didn't fall out.

'I'm going outside,' I said, without stopping to pad out my feet with thick knitted socks. I went out of the door, down the driveway, and turned right at the road, keeping my head up. I started running. The baggy boots flapped noisily around my calves and gulped under the arches of my feet. I kept going, down the road, around the corner, along a cleared track towards the woods and the wilds where the snow lay undisturbed. The snow was deep and my feet sunk in great soft drifts as I battled my way through.

And then I couldn't go any further. By now the hurt had turned into a fit of fury – ungratefulness has a way of morphing your genuine hurt feelings, like alchemy – and without Mum there to hear my despair and let me unburden myself, I kicked out at a bank of snow against a rockface, thinking it would be something solid to hit against. Instead it began to disintegrate. In my frustration, I took off the boot and flung it as hard as I could. It shot straight up in the air, spinning, hitting a brittle branch. The branch snapped, fell with the boot, and landed on the bank of snow. The bank of snow now cracked and slid, all at once, tumbling down like a miniature avalanche, burying the boot.

I sank down in a cold drift of snow. The hat slipped over my eyes and the fur stuck to my tears. I sobbed noisily, hunched over in the puffy coat like a bawling brown boulder.

CHAPTER SIX

It so happened that quite a few months earlier, and a long way from Norway, an iron gate, normally bolted and padlocked, had been left open. The gate was the only way out of a small concrete and metal-barred enclosure where a bear had been caged for many, many years. It took the fragile old brown bear only seconds to notice that he could leave, but long-held fear and conditioning made him falter.

As a bear cub, he'd had an older sister with whom

he had played in their cave while their mother fished the salmon rivers or foraged for berries. The bear cub would cry at first until his sister comforted him. As he grew bolder, he wandered, curious about the world and the place he would have in it, until one day a dangerous new smell touched his nose. At a distance, his sister called from where she had shinned part way up a tree, wailing the alarm for her brother to come back. The little bear returned hastily, the smell he was alert to growing stronger. There were humans around the tree. Bear never forgot that smell nor the sequence of sounds that followed. His small but powerful nose smelled metal, gunpowder, although he did not know what they were. And he smelled fear too, but it was mostly not his or his sister's. He did not know that what he then heard was the slide of a cartridge into a gun, and a long, slow ease of metal with an unmistakable *click*. A pause before a violent *crack* split the air. A burning smell. A soft *thump* as his sister fell from the tree.

The bear cub ran towards the people surrounding the tree but he was too late. He stood on his hind legs but he had no roar yet. They laughed at him; how small he was, how weakly he cried. They netted the little bear, tied him up and carried him away.

The bear cub was chained to a post and made to dance when they played music or clapped and sang. He stood up on his hind legs but had to stop crying out or else the iron bar would sting him when he didn't want to dance. The people who had tied him only saw him as something to entertain them, but they forgot about him when they became bored. Bear grew big but so did his fear. He grew in fear of humans and their metal sticks. He behaved as they made him, subdued by emptiness, cowered in fright.

Later, he was used by militants to carry their weapons, harnessed to a trailer weighed down with a machine gun. Muzzled and chained, he carried their heavy loads, trembling from the *crack* and *boom* of guns in the mountains that reminded him again and again that he was powerless against humans. When the fighting was over, he was once again tied to a post and made to dance, still afraid and all alone. They grew bored once again, and he grew old.

But the power to be what he was, his true nature, would always be there, no matter how deeply denied. The day the open gate to his cage beckoned, the bear still feared what might be outside his jail, and although it made him hesitate, he smelled the late autumn air of the distant mountains. Cautiously, he stepped through the gate. The place was deserted. Although his legs were unused to running, he was free.

He roamed further and further, crossing country borders that no bear or other animal recognizes. His nose drew him to the aroma of berries and to dig up roots from deep in the earth, but he had not been with his family long enough to be properly taught to hunt or forage. Winter came. For so long the bear had been away from his natural habitat that he didn't know where to find the food he needed to maintain his great body. Hunger and the cold call of winter sleep overcame him. He found himself a cave to shelter from the snow and lay down. He fell deeply asleep.

A bank of snow built up over winter creating a thick cover across the entrance to the cave until one day, the week before Christmas, a flying boot and a loose branch from a nearby tree knocked that snow door away.

The old bear's mighty nose had been tucked into his thick fur coat. His heart rate had slowed. With little reserves to keep him alive he would have died before the spring if he hadn't, by mistake, been woken.

When the snow fell away from his cave entrance, it allowed the air from outside to tumble in. Pine. Damp wood. Evergreens. And the scent of a human, crying noisily.

CHAPTER SEVEN

After breakfast the next day, Henry's new family all did their own things. Inge ran a bakery, so she left the house at some horribly early hour, and Elissa had gone to a friend's house. They were quite an independent bunch, whereas my life had always been intertwined with Mum's. Holed up in Hess's room, I was still stewing badly over the birthday present. Without the typewriter, the words I had imagined typing about my reunion with Henry in Norway were as blank as the white snow. Even though the winter scene outside was more festive than anything I'd ever seen, inside Henry's house it felt like Christmas was missing. I decided to ask him if we could go and choose a tree, and maybe that would give me the chance to be alone with him.

Henry poked his head into my room. I was ready to announce my plan. 'Christmas is coming,' I said, as cheerfully as I could.

'And I've got to go to work,' Henry said.

'But—'

'Lars will show you around.'

He left in his van for the studio where he made furniture. That second day in Norway, Lars and I were abandoned to ourselves. They were very relaxed about leaving us back in those days, especially in such a quiet, out-of-the-way place, but all I was left with was the feeling of resentment at having been overlooked for something made of wood.

Lars was doing something in the workshop. He kept coming in and out of the house, kicking off his boots to get a drink from the kitchen, using the bathroom, slowly walking past my open bedroom door, sometimes lingering by the doorway pretending he was looking for something. Each time he brought with him a block of wood that he must have been thinking about working on. I knew he was trying to get my attention but I didn't want to give it to him.

Lars came inside the house and up the stairs yet again. He poked his head into my room and this time stopped to ask me what I was doing.

'I'm busy,' I told Lars, my back to him.

Lars sighed. 'I'm going to be in the workshop. Do you want to come and help me instead?'

I could have spit! Not only had Henry palmed me off with wellies, now I was stuck with someone who rivalled me for Henry's attention. I decided to call Mum to tell her I wanted to come home.

'Can I use the phone, please?' I said.

'We're only supposed to use the phone in the evenings . . .' I turned and glared at him. 'But I'm sure Inge won't mind,' he said. It peeved me that he continued to call his mother by her first name but even more so that he didn't mention if Henry would or wouldn't mind. Wasn't it his house too?

'Where *is* the phone?' I said, intending to have a very long and expensive phone call.

Lars showed me where it was downstairs, and then hung around. 'It's private,' I said, huffing until he went away.

I phoned Mum and told her the news that I had been given a pair of rubber boots instead of a typewriter. I told her I missed her. She told me she missed me too. I couldn't say that Henry showed no interest in me whatsoever. It was too painful to admit.

'I've already got writer's block and I haven't even

started being a proper writer. I made a mistake asking for a typewriter.' I thought she would agree to whisk me back home again.

From the other end of the phone I could tell Mum was disappointed too, but she didn't want me to give up so quickly on what I wanted to be.

'You can use these feelings to write,' she said. 'Isn't it a writer's job to investigate your emotions to understand how to write stories about them?' She avoided talking about any issues surrounding Henry. 'As you were given boots, why don't you take the opportunity to go out and explore. There's a forest nearby, isn't there? Perhaps you can find a different kind of inspiration, maybe from your new surroundings.'

The boot I'd kicked off was still in the woods. I'd been in such a miserable state that I'd left it there and had limped back to the house with a soaked and freezing foot once the sobbing had stopped. Nobody had noticed and nobody had said anything when I went straight to my room saying I was tired. I didn't want the boots, but with only one boot I might end up stuck in the house. I didn't want to own up to how I'd lost it. Henry would think I was a stroppy child and Inge would think me plain rude.

'There's only snow out there,' I said. 'It's just white.' I didn't mean it. I only wanted to go home and be with Mum.

'What about going into town? You could write about the things you discover there.'

I couldn't even admit to Mum that I had only half a pair of boots, but she was soothing and wise and I listened.

At Mum's suggestion I decided to take the snow-cleared route into town and snuck out in my trainers, with my satchel, while Lars was on another visit to the workshop. But my trainers proved to be more than useless in protecting me from the cold and although the small town wasn't far, my shoes and socks were soon soaked through, my feet stinging and squelching, and the wet was creeping up the legs of my jeans. I also had the creepy feeling I was being followed. I kept looking over my shoulder but all the people I could see were going about their shopping, coming in and out of shop doors. I was hardly inconspicuous in the puffy jacket-potato coat, furry hat and inappropriate trainers if anyone *was* trying to follow me, but I couldn't shake the feeling of being watched and ducked into an alleyway. I stopped and peered around the side. From a doorway on the other side of the road a head poked out with a hat and pasta hair. Lars!

My first thought was that he would notice I wasn't wearing the boots and he would tell Inge. I sneaked further along the snow-cleared alley and hid in the doorway of a shop with coloured fairy lights outlining the window and silver tinsel wrapped around a signpost on which was painted *Årgang*.

I was about to run on before Lars could see where I went, when I saw something that convinced me to go into the shop instead. An old typewriter was displayed in the window.

CHAPTER EIGHT

Årgang meant vintage. The shop spilled over with old, used and second-hand things. The shelves on the back wall were stacked with random flower-painted teacups and saucers, dishes, bowls and glass vases, not many of which were from the same set. Festooned with Christmas lights, the shop had chandeliers dangling with baubles and paper snowflakes twirling on string hung from the ceiling. I felt as if I had stepped into a Christmas that was as familiar as home.

I shuffled between the rails of long evening gowns and wide-shouldered coats on hangers, hiding between them for a moment in case Lars looked through the window, before making my way to the back of the shop where I came across the owner. She wore scarlet lipstick, her glossy dark hair curled neatly at the side of her face. Her dress was from the 1940s, she wore high heels and held a thin black cigarette holder between her teeth. I couldn't stop staring. For a moment I thought I had stepped into an old movie.

'*Velkommen*,' she said, taking the cigarette holder from her mouth and blowing into the air. No smoke came out.

'I am just looking,' I said, pronouncing the words clearly, pointing to my eyes and then my chest. 'I am English.'

'I speak English,' she said. 'And I'm flattered that you've come such a long way to visit my shop.' She bent to pick up a lead and plugged it into a socket.

'It's not real,' she said. 'The cigarette, I mean. It's just for effect.'

'Sorry, I didn't mean to stare.'

I noticed a big sign at the rear of the shop, saying, *I Do Not Buy or Sell Furs!* and slipped the rabbit-fur hat from my head. I was stuffing it in my pocket when she strode over and caught my hand. She rubbed the fur between her fingers.

'Fake,' she said. 'Thin and floozy, unlike the real thing.'

'Oh!' I was a little taken aback by her boldness, but relieved not to have offended her with my hat.

'It's not necessary to be cruel when we have developed so many marvellous fabrics.' She plucked a beaded dress from the rail and swung it in front of her. She twirled with it. 'You see?'

The slight movement of air stirred the decorations and in that moment the beads and baubles twinkled as they reflected the lights and came alive with the woman and the dress.

'It's beautiful,' I said.

'I'm glad we understand each other.' She smiled, as if pleased at my reaction rather than the dress itself, and clipped the hanger back on the rail. 'Now, you need to get dry, my darling.'

She pulled up a chair in front of the electric fire she'd plugged in, which had already begun to turn orange and smelled of singed dust, and told me to sit and take off my shoes and socks. I must have looked a sorry sight and was grateful for the welcome and warmth.

'What can I interest you in?' she said, gesturing elegantly with her hand.

'I came in because I saw the typewriter,' I said, feeling as dull as a root vegetable beside an exotic flower.

'I thought you'd come in for a pair of boots.' She laughed and her eyelashes fluttered.

I looked down at my sodden trainers and sighed.

'The typewriter is a 1958 Hermes 3000, an

absolute classic,' she said. 'Want a closer look?'

'Yes, please!' She was right that I needed some boots though. There were quite a few pairs in the shop, worn into the remembered shape of their previous owners' feet. I'd been given a wearable pair of boots (well, I had one of them and knew roughly where the other one was), and I knew I could hardly walk about in my trainers. But just then I only had eyes for the typewriter.

The overflowing shop was difficult to navigate and she passed me a short stepladder.

'I shan't be climbing in heels, my darling,' she said. 'Can you reach it?'

I climbed, leaned over the rails, and picked up the typewriter from the tall stand in the window. I sat on the platform at the top of the ladder with the typewriter on my lap and felt at home with it right away. The Hermes 3000 was pale green, the black letters in a simple clean style on square but round-edged keys. It was even older than the one

Mum had been bringing home to teach me to type.

I gave it a try but the metal bars with the letters on the end tangled together.

'It needs a little practice to get a feel for how it works, and maybe a squirt of oil,' the woman said.

I warmed with the attention she gave me and the atmosphere in the shop. She was the first person in Norway who made me feel invited in *and* who was acknowledging my writing. I sensed myself opening up a little. I must have closed my heart tightly since I'd arrived.

'My mum has been teaching me to type because I want to be a writer,' I told her while she offered me sheets of paper and I fed one into the roller. I almost mentioned the fact that I hadn't received the present I was hoping for, but the thought of Henry made it feel far too raw to mention.

I looked at the price tag on the typewriter, took my purse out of my satchel and counted my money, even though it was meant for buying

Henry a Christmas present while I was there. I didn't have anywhere near enough for the typewriter.

'Never mind,' she said, seeing me close my purse. 'While you are here, why don't you have another little go?'

The touch of those keys was magic to me. I typed:

```
My name is Thea Whittington, aged
12, and I want to be a writer.
```

The shop owner leaned over to read it. She told me to call her V.

'It's short for Victory.' She smiled. 'Not really, but wouldn't that be good if it was true? Actually it's Valda, but call me V if you feel like being my friend.'

She made me feel relaxed, as if she was only playing with everything, even her name. It was a relief after how stiff and uncomfortable everything was at Henry's.

'Okay, V,' I said, excited by her invitation.

'How does the typewriter feel, Thea Whittington?'

I rested the tips of my fingers on the middle line, as Mum had taught me, where finger-shaped grooves were softly moulded into them. I felt more myself in that moment than I had since leaving home. 'It feels like it fits me.'

V nodded slowly, as if she sensed some kind of connection and it pleased her. It made me feel confident enough to ask a favour.

'Would you mind if I came back and borrowed the typewriter while I'm in the shop? I'd like to write a story about my holiday while I'm staying here,' I said, explaining it would only be for a week.

V said yes, I could come into the shop anytime I liked. 'I think I would very much enjoy the company of a writer in residence,' she said, adding, however, that if anyone came in to buy the typewriter she would have to sell it. 'In the meantime, it's yours to use whenever you want.'

Mum was right about how the writer in me needed to investigate and explore, and I thought it was this part of me that I needed to show Henry. Restored by the thought of using the typewriter, the possibility of writing my reunion story about us still seemed open. I wondered if he might even consider buying me the Hermes 3000 for Christmas. I stayed for a little while, typing up my journey and arrival in Norway and my meeting with V.

When I left the shop, my shoes were soon soaked again and my feet frozen, and I decided the first sensible thing I had to do was to retrieve the missing boot. Whether I liked the boots or not, trips to V's shop didn't need to involve painful toes.

I was headed back towards the house when I spied Lars, crouched behind a wall on the other side of the road. He'd lost me in town but I guessed he knew eventually I'd have to come back this way. His perseverance in waiting so long was sort of admirable, I had to at least give him that.

Lars jumped out. 'Where did you go?'

'Into town,' I said, irritated by his jack-in-a-box presence.

'Where are your boots?' he asked suspiciously.

I marched ahead. 'Nowhere special.'

'Shall I tell Inge about them?' he called.

'Go ahead!' Now I had no choice but to find the boot before he snitched on me.

CHAPTER NINE

First, though, I needed to shake off Lars again. I decided to head back to the house to change my wet socks. My feet were stinging again and were good enough reason by themselves to make me go looking for the boot as soon as I could. Lars followed me to my room. I shut the door. It was only then that I saw he'd left balled pairs of thick socks on the end of my bed. I suddenly felt completely out of sorts for being so mean to him. It wasn't how I usually would be.

I could tell Lars had his face pressed against the door because his voice was muffled as he kept asking me what I was doing while my trainers dried on the radiator.

'I know you're not doing anything,' Lars said, his voice still close to the door. 'And Inge says I have to make you come and do something with me today.'

'What exactly is it you're doing?' I muttered.

'I've got some wood and I'm trying to think of ideas for something to make. I would like an assistant.'

'I'm busy!' He might have been useful with the socks but he was also annoyingly in my way.

He was quiet for a moment. 'It's because you can't do it and because you don't know anything about using wood to make things.' And then he added sulkily, 'Inge will be mad at me for leaving you on your own.'

As long as Inge was mad with Lars, then I could live with that. But I realized I would need a different tactic if I was going to find the boot without him knowing.

'Okay, I'll come. I'll be there in a few minutes when I've put some warmer socks on.'

'I'll be in the workshop,' he said, and I heard him happily jumping downstairs.

What I needed was a shovel to help me dig the missing boot out of the snow. I guessed that they must have a snow shovel because the driveway had been cleared and it was most likely in the workshop or garage. I put on a pair of Lars's thick socks and my trainers and went outside with the one boot I had zipped inside my coat, wearing my satchel across my chest to disguise how lumpy it was. I soon spotted a wide shovel leaning against the wall inside the workshop door.

Lars seemed pleased I was there. He wandered around the workshop, picking things up and putting them back down, saying, 'I'm not sure what to make. I have some ideas, but . . .'

I was taking almost no notice of anything he said about chipping and sawing bits of wood with certain tools, or of anything in the workshop except the tantalizing shovel. I waited as long as I could bear (about four minutes) before saying I needed to pop back inside the house to use the loo. When his back was turned, I slipped the shovel in front of my body. As I walked towards the front door of the house, I swerved quickly, ducked my head below the piled-up snow along the driveway (I could hear Lars humming to himself, so I knew he was distracted) and sprinted off up the road towards the woods and the wilds before he could notice.

My footprints from the previous miserable visit were still pierced in the smooth snow – actually they were more like leg holes as the snow was so soft and deep – and I used the shovel like a walking stick to help me clamber through the drifts. I was thinking about how Henry and I might spend time together. Maybe we could go into town and I could pick him a Christmas present. Or maybe I could ask him to take me exploring in places like this, secret places we would remember as ours, or he could show me special trees where we'd carve our initials, or tell me old Norwegian tales of woodsmen and their daughters, something I really wanted to write about and for him to read. In my imagination it all felt possible now I knew where to find a typewriter.

It hadn't snowed since the day before and the tree with the broken branch was easy to spot where the green pine needles had been exposed. The end of the fallen branch was sticking out of a mound of snow where I knew the boot must be buried.

The woods and the wilds were perfectly quiet. I began to dig and the only sound was the *swoosh* of the shovel as it sliced through the snow. I thought I heard something else and stopped for a second to listen. My first thought was that Lars might have followed me. I crouched down low so that he wouldn't be able to see me, but the sound had stopped. I peeked up carefully. Nobody appeared. I continued digging but heard it again – a little crackling of ice and shuffling in the snow, and a loud sort of puffing. It came from close by.

'Lars! Are you hiding?' I called out, as much to make myself feel more confident as anything else.

The toe of the boot was now exposed and I wanted to snatch it up and make a run for it, but before I could, a huge dark shape rose from behind the bank of snow.

A great brown bear, as wide as three people, as tall as two, stood on its back legs and towered over me. It opened its jaws and snarled.

In shock, I froze, and for a moment stood there thinking only that I must be about to die. I had stopped breathing, but I could hear the bear's dry rough breath and sniffing nose. Why hadn't anyone told me there were bears? Why hadn't Henry cared enough to warn me? I was going to die and never become a writer. I closed my eyes.

But nothing happened.

No roaring, no pain; nothing charged at me or engulfed me.

Only my nostrils quivered with a smell like old damp carpet.

I opened my eyes.

The bear was on all fours now, its head low, looking towards me. It shifted from side to side, not more than three metres away. I didn't know what to do. A strangled moan seeped from my throat. The bear backed away from me.

Its fearful demeanour was so surprising that I just stared – at the gold fur over its snout, bare in patches, at its juicy big blackberry nose, and the shallow curve of its quivering lips. Gold-tipped fur crowned its head, edged the ruff around its throat and the frown between its eyes. I noticed the ragged fur on the bear's belly and the jut of

its angular hips and shoulders. There were rings of dark bare skin around its leg and I could not help but think its lowered head and tentative watch made it seem scared and unhappy. But however unhappy or scared the bear might be, I knew I was in danger. All I could think to do was to hold up my hand like a traffic policeman directing a truck to halt.

'I need my boot, I really do,' I said gently, so as not to alarm or provoke it. 'I am going to be in so much trouble. And I'm not normally in trouble.

It's just that things are . . . well, I'm not exactly happy right now. Understand?' I had no idea why I was saying it or what I was doing, but my hand seemed to miraculously signal to the bear to remain where he was.

'Good bear,' I said. 'You stay there. I'll get the boot and then I'll go.'

I reached for the boot and pulled it out of the snow and, as I did, the bear raised its paw to me too. I stopped. It filled my heart with pure wonder to see such a rare creature as this but I was stunned as it seemed such a strange thing for a wild bear to do. And while I seemed to have an inkling that all was not well with the bear, all my other worries had completely vanished.

But it was an enormous brown bear after all, and I needed to escape.

CHAPTER TEN

I backed away, taking care not to move suddenly. My heart raced and all my senses were alert. I kept my eyes on the bear the whole time, anticipating the distance I'd need when it might be safe for me to run. But the strangest thing was that at no point did the bear look as if it might make chase. In fact, it backed away behind a tree, and then edged out a little, watching me go. I could not make sense of such a giant looking at me as if it were a mouse and I a cat.

When I had made my escape back to the road, I ran, hopping along trying to put the boots on, stuff the trainers in my satchel and keep moving at the same time. I'd left the shovel behind. Without really thinking what I was doing, I ran all the way to V's shop in town instead of returning to the house. I suppose I had already thought of the shop with the typewriter and the shining chandelier as a haven of some sort.

I went inside and stood with my back to the door, panting. I could hear an agitated customer talking to V. A man, younger than Henry, wearing a checked jacket, glanced over at me. He wore a similar hat to the one Inge had given me, with red ear-flaps tied over the top of his shoulder-length blond hair. He finished his conversation and, as I stepped forward, pushed past me in the narrow space between the rails to hurry out of the door. I leaned back to get out of his path but the hangers of soft clothes gave way and I slipped through and landed on the floor on my behind. The man said something in Norwegian to me and then the door closed behind him with a *thump*.

'Oh, that beastly man!' V sighed. 'Thea? Where are you, darling?' She pushed the hangers apart and crouched down. 'I'm sorry. That was Mr Prag. He's one of our town councillors and rather pompous for one so young. Are you okay?' She held out her hands and pulled me upright. 'Nice warm boots,' she said, nodding towards my feet.

I looked down. *Are they?* I was unable to make sense of anything for a moment. Alone with V, the after-effects of shock set in and I began to shiver and shake.

'Where have you just come from?' V said, obviously concerned at my demeanour.

'The woods.'

'Are you okay, darling?'

'It's all right; I'm not hurt.' I said it as much to tell myself that I really was miraculously okay.

I was unwilling to tell V what had happened, embarrassed that I might have done something as stupid as to go to the woods while there were bears around. Would I also be in trouble if I had to explain that I was there because I'd thrown one of the boots away? I was safe. Did anyone need to know? I told V I had got cold and she sat me in front of the fire again.

My head was full of what had happened. I didn't know much about bears, nor that they lived in Norway, and I couldn't understand why Henry or the family wouldn't have warned me if they knew that a bear lived not far from their house. But although it had been me who had been vulnerable, I couldn't escape the strange, implausible feeling that the bear had needed help more than I had.

'What do you know about bears?' I asked V. 'I mean, what should I do if I see one?'

'Are you a town girl?' I nodded. 'No need to worry. There are very few bears in Norway, and it would be highly unusual to see one around here, especially at this time of year. Bears hibernate in the winter and prefer to avoid humans at all costs.' She hesitated a moment before going on. 'It's extremely unlikely you'll meet one in the woods, if that's what you have been scaring yourself about.'

I didn't want anyone to worry, and knowing I'd had a lucky and unusual encounter I tried to put it to one side until I could think clearly about it all. I picked up a teddy bear from a shelf for distraction.

'This bear looks very used,' I said.

'Everything in my shop has had a previous life elsewhere. Isn't it wonderful to know it has been owned and loved already?'

'Isn't it better if you're the first person to have something?' I said, putting the teddy back on the shelf, thinking of Henry being my father first, before anyone else's, especially Lars's.

'But why? Does it matter to you if somebody used the Hermes 3000 before you?'

V had a wonderful way of making me think without interfering in my thinking. The typewriter was back in the window and I retrieved it again with the help of the stepladder and sat with it on my lap for comfort. I wondered if a crime writer had owned the typewriter before and maybe even left their fingerprints on the keys. It added to the importance of the typewriter, made me feel as if I was connected to other storytellers. My heart swelled at the thought of using the same keys as a real writer might have done.

'No, I don't suppose so. Actually, it makes it more special, somehow.'

V seemed to like that I said that. 'Are you sure you're okay? You still look a little peaky. How about I make us a nice cup of sweet tea?'

V made a pot and used two cups and saucers from a shelf in the shop. A small v-shaped crack spoiled the smoothness of the rim of the cup she gave me and a ring was still visible on the saucer, as if a plant pot had stood on it for a long time.

'I still remember the good strong tea and conversations my mother and I used to share over these cups.' She poured tea and milk and added several spoons of sugar to mine. 'Using them makes me feel as if she's still here.' I think I understood. It was similar to how I believed a story would create a connection between me and Henry.

'So why are you selling them?'

'I'm not, and I wouldn't. I like to think something of her company remains, somewhere in the pores of the china, perhaps. And for me, that makes them priceless.' She winked at me, sipped and placed her cup gently back in the saucer. She looked down at the floor for a moment with what looked like sadness. 'I kept lots of her things.'

The sweet tea revived us. I placed my cup and saucer on the shelf beside the old teddy bear and took a good look at it.

The bear hinged at the shoulders and hips. I brushed its worn face and polished its glass eyes with my sleeve and bent the joints, stiff with age, so the bear was in a sitting position, one paw raised, like the one I'd seen in the woods and the wilds. I imagined the many cuddles and the many nights the teddy had spent tucked in someone's arms, the comforting snuffle of its ears or ribbon under someone's nose.

'What if the person who owned the teddy bear just left it on a shelf?'

V shrugged. 'I think you can tell,' she said. She picked it up and with her head tilted to one side had a good look too. 'Definitely worn from love.'

The bear in the woods had seemed hollow though, worn out, but I didn't think from love. Why had it looked this way? It had seemed to want to avoid me. And it should have been hibernating.

'Are you thinking of writing a story about bears?' V asked.

'Maybe,' I said.

I thought V was right about the teddy bear but I wasn't sure about the bear in the woods at all. Why had it woken up? Why had it seemed so . . . lost? What was missing from the story I wanted to know and be able to tell? My fingers tapped restlessly against the keys.

V meanwhile had found an antique book on her shelves with lots of photographs of Norwegian wildlife. 'You could look at these pictures for inspiration.'

There was only a little text in the book next to a photo of a group of well-stuffed brown bears fishing for salmon in a river. V was happy to translate what it said and she told me the little she knew about bears, although she had never seen one in the wild.

'Bears are all about the food and what they are filled with.' She plumped up the sawdust in the teddy bear a little. 'If they are full, if they have plenty, they feel content.'

Was that what had happened to my bear? (I was already thinking of him as mine.) I started to type, my fingers remembering where some of the letters lived. I wrote about everything that had happened since yesterday, and all that had happened today. I had little to say about Henry and me, but a lot to say about the bear. Everything disappeared except my story.

CHAPTER ELEVEN

I couldn't stop thinking about the bear. Judging by the difference in size and shape of male and female bears in the photographs in V's book, the one I had seen was male. His hollowed belly told me that perhaps he hadn't found enough food to sleep soundly. Or perhaps he had smelled me and thought I was food! I tried to piece together what I thought I had seen. It grew into a kind of loose map of who the bear might be and why he looked the way he did. I could not help picturing his expression as I'd left him – he had seemed so human, so like me.

It's not every day you come face to face with such an astonishing and large animal like that. The bear had not hurt me, and in fact had done exactly as I asked; and although I could not fathom exactly why that might have been, it was an extremely encouraging thought. I wondered how life had led us to meet in the way we had. If V was right, that a full bear was a happy bear, then maybe I could help fill his belly. But was it just food he needed? I wanted to know so much more about him. I needed to see him again. If I had understood then the risks involved in encountering a wild bear, I don't think I would have gone back to find him, and neither would anyone have let me if I had told them what had happened. In fact, the whole story may have turned out entirely differently. As it was, I was fuelled by a very strong passion not only to write a story, but to be part of it too.

I folded the sheets of my story that I had typed so far, put them in my satchel, and headed back to the house, which was dark in the gloom of the cloudy afternoon. Inside, the only light came from around Lars where he was staring into the open fridge. I had forgotten all about leaving him earlier, and for a moment I felt a pang of guilt. He saw me out of the corner of his eye and started humming to make it seem like he was interested in what was on the fridge shelves rather than me. He was obviously upset with me but I fixed a fierce frown on my face so that he wouldn't think it a good idea to ask where I'd been.

If I wanted to take some food for the bear, I needed to disguise what I was doing.

'Am I allowed to get something to eat?' I took a jar from the fridge with pale jelly in it, opened the lid and sniffed. It wasn't marmalade, or anything I could identify.

'Spruce jelly.' I raised my eyebrows and stared

back. 'Inge makes it from spruce leaves. Henry likes it with cheese,' he said.

I closed the lid and plonked it back on the shelf.

'We were supposed to make a cheese sandwich for lunch.' He showed me a block of something brown. My nose instinctively turned up. I didn't think I'd like brown cheese, and I wasn't sure if a bear would either.

'Is there anything else?'

Lars seemed relieved to find that he could have a slightly easier conversation with me than one about helping him to make something out of wood or where I'd been. He took a dish from the fridge and peeled back the foil cover.

'We could have meatballs.' He looked satisfied with what he could offer me but I'd not come across meatballs before and wasn't quite sure what they tasted like. I probably frowned or pulled a face, so Lars picked one up and popped it whole in his mouth. He heaved another dish out. 'Or salmon fish?' His cheek ballooned with the meatball.

From a cupboard he opened a bag of salted crisps and held it out, immediately pulling it away before I had a chance to put my hand in, and emptied some into a bowl. He'd probably been told to be polite and treat me like a guest. I didn't want to think of any of them as family, except Henry, but I resented being treated like a guest too. There really was no pleasing my sooty heart.

He shut the fridge door and with the bright light gone we were left in the gloom. At home, our house would be glowing warmly with multicoloured Christmas lights.

'Why don't you have any Christmas decorations?' I took a handful of crisps, momentarily distracted.

'It isn't Christmas yet,' he mumbled through the meatball.

'Yes, but *we* don't just do it for Christmas Day.' Of course, I meant *my own people*, like Mum and me, who understood Christmas in the same way, which separated me from the people who happened to currently be Henry's so-called family. '*We* have strings of baubles and tinsel and a special star which plugs in.'

I intended to show Lars our differences, I guess because I wanted some kind of proof that *my* version of the family had been somehow better than his.

'Our star has lights around it,' I continued, stuffing crisps in my mouth. 'And it's painted silver.'

'We don't have one of those.' His voice sounded pasty. He kept chewing, trying to swallow. The meatball was dry and he coughed. I don't think he knew quite why I was so mad at him but I'd made my point and wiped the salt from my fingers with a clap of my hands.

After he'd recovered with a glass of water, I said, 'I'd like some fish, lots of fish,' prompted by V's book.

Seeming relieved that I had changed the subject,

Lars cut two huge slices from the cooked salmon, leaving a small piece in the dish, and scooped our portions on to two plates. He got forks and knives from the drawer and carried them to the table. Without taking off my coat I sat, twiddled the fork and waited while he ate, hoping to put Lars off the scent of what I was really up to.

'After lunch I could show you Henry's cabin,' he said.

'Henry's cabin?' This was news to me. It was the sort of thing that Henry should have told me and shown me, food for writing about.

'He goes there to be on his own sometimes.'

I felt slightly satisfied at first that Henry wanted to avoid Inge and her family, but the feeling didn't last, as I remembered he'd also gone off to be on his own when he'd been with Mum and me.

'Do you want to see it?' Lars said. 'It's not too far.'

I narrowed my eyes. I would have liked Henry to have taken me, not Lars. It felt like hand-me-down information that I would have loved to have come to me fresh from Henry when we spent time together. But more than anything now I wanted to get away from how awful I felt about it all and go to the bear who was nothing to do with any of it. I put the fork down.

'Actually, I've changed my mind about the food because I'm not hungry yet and I'm extremely busy anyway.' I got up, took the plate with me and went out of the door, leaving Lars sitting at the table.

CHAPTER TWELVE

I n the woods and the wilds, the ground was frozen as hard as iron, the trees held still in time, and yet my senses felt wider awake than I'd ever known, alert to the soft contours and ice-blue shadows, and the bright clean scent. Infused with the fragrance and stillness of evergreen winter it was quiet, like nothing I'd ever heard before. My heart, however, was thumping hard as I approached the place where I'd seen the bear. I hoped he would still be there, or at least close by, as there were no footprints of his that I could see.

From what V's book had told me, a bear's nose was extremely powerful, so I was unnerved, cautious about him smelling me from afar. But there was a clear view between the trees and I thought I could hide at a distance and watch the bear without putting myself in danger.

I crouched and scooped a hole with gloved hands, dropping a piece of salmon in the pocket, as I had in other places nearby, and filled it back up with snow before retreating. I hoped I could entice the bear with the food to walk around and do bear-like things so I could safely study him some more.

Almost everything was shades of white, except for me in the potato coat and rabbit-eared hat, and then, all of a sudden, the gold-crowned bear who appeared nearby.

The same overwhelming shock at his size and presence hit me and my desire was overpowered by the fear that with one swipe of his great paw I might never be seen again.

I sucked myself in behind the tree, peeping out quickly to see if he was coming for me. His nose twitched in my direction. I couldn't be sure if he had smelled or seen me because he remained where he was. But then *he* stepped back behind a tree as if he had sensed something and was unsure.

I could not take my eyes off him, as, like me, he peered out too. Was this a game?

I could hardly believe my eyes when he raised his paw in my direction, just as he had done before. I instinctively raised my own hand, peeping out so he could see I was waving too. Was this a usual bear thing? Encouraged, I stepped out a little, and, as if this invited the bear, he did too! His nose glistened as he watched me, waiting.

I pointed away from me, where the fish was buried. I stepped sideways to persuade the bear to move towards where I was pointing. The bear took a step. He seemed as interested in copying me as he was in the scent which made his nose twitch. *Had he been taught to do this?* I wondered. I stored it all for writing later.

I wafted my arms in the direction I wanted the bear to go. Suddenly he charged, barrelling like a tank through the snow. Alarmed, I grabbed a fallen stick, only to see that he was taking a wide berth around me and running towards the food. As he saw me wield the stick, he skidded to a halt and stumbled backwards, hunched as if to draw himself in smaller. I could not fathom what was happening, except that I saw in him what I felt in myself. I was afraid he'd hurt me but he seemed just as afraid that I might hurt him. How could something as enormous as he was have so much fear?

The bear snorted, his lips quivering, his feet shuffling. I dropped the stick.

'Is your nose telling you something?' I wanted to calm and reassure him and his agitated movements remarkably stopped on hearing my voice. 'I've brought you some fish to eat. Do you like fish? Really, you can go and get the food. I brought it for you. You only have to follow your nose.'

I too took a wide berth around him, to put space between us. Over by the disturbed bank of snow, where the boot had been buried, I hid myself in the contours of the rockface, humming sweetly so he knew where I was and to tell him that I was just going about my business and letting him have the food all to himself. Beside me, I noticed a deep shadow and the entrance of a cave. I guessed it must have been the place where the bear had been hibernating.

The bear made his way to the scented map of buried fish which I hoped would remind him of rivers rushing with wriggling autumn salmon, *if* he was as wild as the bears in V's book. He dug small trenches, pushing his claws and his nose into the holes, before scooping out the fish. He licked flakes off his paws, all the while looking over at me as if to check that I was still there, that he was still safe.

He made me smile, digging and grunting and licking between each claw for every tiny iridescent scale, watching me now and then. I could see little sign of his wildness but I was completely drawn into the wondrous rare treat of watching the bear savouring his food.

'I was going to write about me and my dad on my holiday.' I spoke gently. 'He's called Henry . . . but, well, he's not here so I'm going to write about you instead, Bear, because you definitely are. I hope you don't mind.' It didn't feel strange talking to the bear. In fact, I liked very much hearing my own voice, full of affection for my discovery, instead of my bad-tempered manner with Lars when he probably hadn't really deserved it. I forgot all my problems while the bear licked his chops.

When the bear had fished out all the salmon from the holes, he sat down and seemed to study me. Was he still hungry? Perhaps he was looking at me too intently now.

I retreated as the short day drew to a close and although I shivered at the thought of what I had just done, I noticed something in myself for the first time since I'd arrived in Norway. The bear had made me feel content.

CHAPTER THIRTEEN

My mind and heart burned brightly with wonder. I felt the bear and I had formed some kind of bond. As soon as I left him, I was planning to go back. I needed more food for him. I wanted more of how he made me feel, to know more about him, and I was overflowing with the things I wanted to write about.

I arrived back at Henry and Inge's house as it was turning dark. While I had been out, the Christmas spirit had still not entered and neither Henry nor sparkle nor lights invited me back into their home.

Two places were laid on one side of the long table for Henry and Inge, three on the other for the children. This was where they usually sat but I had other ideas when Inge called from the kitchen that dinner was ready. I rushed to the table and sat next to Henry, to be beside him.

I thought it wise to not mention the bear. It felt like something private and precious that I was still making sense of. Besides which it would have also involved admitting that my encounter had taken place after flinging away the boot. I pushed it all aside to wait until Henry could read about it later. Instead, I turned my attention to resolving the lack of Christmas in the house, intending to ask Henry if we could make a gingerbread house as we had when I was very small. Mum and I made gingerbread people instead these days, and I, already with a hint of the writer in me, would give the gingerbread people names; characters that I'd invent a story about. I thought it would be nice if Henry and I rekindled this Christmas tradition and he could see why we had changed from making a house to making people. It was one of the few and very special memories I had of us doing something together, and I thought it would help me in my cause to make some kind of connection with him that I felt sure he must remember. Then I'd have an appropriate time to tell him about my writing, maybe mention my handwriting (again) and how much quicker it was for me to type. I could even tell him how I'd found the perfect typewriter at a shop nearby. I was going to be busy the next day. With the bear, with Henry, with the typewriter!

Nobody asked where I'd been but everyone was quieter than I'd already experienced; not an easy quiet, though. Where was their Christmas spirit? I waited for the niggle to pass before I asked Henry.

Inge hesitated when she carried our plates to the

table and saw where I was sitting, but she took the last chair that was left without saying anything. She placed, quite deliberately, a plate with a very small piece of salmon on it in the middle of the table.

Mortified, I realized that we were supposed to be having salmon for dinner. Everyone stared at the measly leftovers like evidence of a crime. There was barely enough for one person. I was glad Henry couldn't see my face when I realized the consequences of what I had done, but to my great surprise, Lars immediately took the blame for the missing salmon. I had no idea why he was doing it but he saved me from the horror of getting found out.

'I'm sorry,' Lars said. Inge responded snappily in Norwegian.

My heart deflated as I sat with everyone around the supper table, each of us with only two forkfuls of salmon but extra helpings of potato dumplings and mashed swede to make up for it. I appreciated

Lars might be nicer than I had thought and had saved me from trouble but I did not feel good at all. Periodically, Elissa and Inge spoke to each other in Norwegian, sharply, with Lars's name being mentioned as they scraped cutlery over crockery. Lars sighed many times; his shoulders drooped but he kept his eyes down and I, unsure what to make of his generosity, kept mine down and avoided eye contact too.

He kept repeating, in English, 'I was just hungry!'

And then Henry said, 'It's only a piece of fish, not the end of the world. But next time have a good breakfast, son.'

My stomach twisted with envy at Henry's use of the word 'son'. He had hardly interacted with me, his own daughter, since I'd arrived here. I shuffled the food around, taking out all my distress on the soft dumplings.

Inge kicked Henry under the table and he looked up suddenly and frowned.

'I'm making something in the workshop. Do you want to see?' Henry asked me.

'Actually, I'm a bit tired. I'd like to go to bed.'

My throat tightened, and I immediately regretted what I'd said. I wanted to go with him, but I was hurt, and I wanted to hurt him back. I quickly escaped upstairs with bitter swede swilling around in my stomach, holding my chin high because tears threatened again.

It was hard to sleep that night, and not only because I started to feel hungry when the sweet smell of browning pastry from a pie that Inge was making wafted up and slipped through the thin gap under the door and into my nose. Later, Henry knocked and opened the door. He stood there for a moment, but I kept my back to him under the covers, too wounded to offer him anything of myself, and he must have assumed I was asleep.

CHAPTER FOURTEEN

All night, I'd been holding on to my regret at refusing Henry's offer. I didn't like feeling like that and I wasn't a quitter. Inge had already left for work, and downstairs Henry, Elissa and Lars were having breakfast at the table. I sat next to Henry again. Putting aside my hurt as much as I could, I took the chance to ask him if he'd make gingerbread with me.

Henry said he and Lars were going logging. 'We need to stock up for the fire. You can come if you want.'

Inwardly trying to bear another rejection, I still couldn't accept the offer on the grounds that I wanted to spend time with Henry but not with Lars.

'But we always used to make a gingerbread house for Christmas. Remember?'

'Elissa likes cooking, don't you?' He got up, nodding to Lars.

Elissa folded her arms and scowled at Henry. He was wrong, she said, she did not like cooking. 'Just because my mother does, it doesn't mean I do!' It surprised me how begrudgingly she spoke to him.

Henry didn't reply and simply left in the van with saws and axes and Lars.

'It's not really cooking, Elissa,' I explained, chin up, as if I knew it all. I was determined to win myself a better position than the one of dismissal that I felt, even though I very much did not want to be passed off on Elissa who wouldn't know what the tradition meant to me. 'It's actually more like carpentry with biscuits.'

If I had stopped for a moment and set my resentment aside, I might have understood what my mother had warned me about before I came to Norway. She'd gently said that Henry had his own interests, and it was unlikely he would change. She had emphasized that I should pursue my dreams of both becoming a writer and finding a way to get closer to Henry, but that I might have to accept he would not, in the end, have a hand in either of these things. But I was not easily thwarted.

'Biscuit carpentry?' Elissa said, rolling her eyes. 'Anyway, I have already arranged to meet my friends at the café.' She looked at me for a long, annoyed moment. 'Do you want to come?' It wasn't a welcoming invitation and I was about to say no when she added, 'You have to come or someone will be cross with me for leaving you on your own.'

I tramped behind her into town while she sauntered ahead, swinging an embroidered cloth bag full of balls of wool and knitting needles.

Before long I found myself sulkily staring out of the window of a café, sitting on the edge of a group of Elissa's friends who had all retrieved wool from their bags. They laughed, chatted and clacked needles while drinking mugs of hot chocolate and whipped cream, paid for out of their own pockets. Why weren't they shopping for Christmas decorations? Why weren't we at the house doing Christmassy things? Why didn't Henry want to do anything with me? I felt separate and dejected, and they probably couldn't have done anything right to my mind.

I recognized pushy Mr Prag who'd been in V's shop, with the red ear-flap hat tied over the top of his head. He was going from table to table (even with his pop-star hair I couldn't understand how he was so popular), stopping for a moment here and there to speak to any adults. I didn't have a drink or knitting and the girls were engrossed in a conversation in Norwegian, so I couldn't even respond huffily because I had no idea what they were saying. Elissa had introduced me by name only, nobody was paying me any attention, and the only one I could think of that had shown me interest was the bear. The minute I recalled him my heart stirred with the magic of being near him. Did he feel neglected in the same way as I did? Was he as out of place here as I was?

I told Elissa I was going for a wander. She said that was fine, as long as I stayed in town, and to come back in an hour. I probably dropped out of her mind in the same way she withered in mine.

Instead of staying in town though, I took the road back to the house.

There was no salmon left in the fridge but Inge had left the pie she had made last night on the side. I looked at it for a long time, wondering whether to take it or not. More than anything I wanted to see the bear, to feel that joy and wonder at something so rare, anything but the misery I felt around Henry's family. It was such a big pie that I felt sure it would help fill the bear up and would give him something that seemed sweetly appropriate in return for how he made me feel. This time I was fully prepared to be found out for taking the pie myself. In fact, I decided that I *wanted* to be found out for taking the family food so that around the table at supper time, and in front of everyone, Henry might say, *It's not the end of the world; it's only a blueberry pie. But, Thea, my dearest daughter, my only real child, next time just ask and you can have whatever you want.*

I felt satisfied I had foretold the outcome and wrapped the pie and put it carefully in my satchel. I wasn't sure if I could rely on what had happened so far to predict that all would be well. Bear was so huge, despite the evidence of loose fur around his bones. I had been lucky twice now to come away unscathed.

No matter how logical the fear, I was desperate to see him, to feel that deep kind of connection. I hoped that the large pie would be sufficient to distract the bear from any ideas of hurting me, but I decided I would spy on him from afar first, to see if I could sense his mood before getting closer.

It had taken the bear months to travel across a vast wilderness to Norway, although his freedom came with a wariness of a world he had all but forgotten.

Had he lived as a bear in the wild he would have known to scare a human off, to make sure when food was scarce that he and his source weren't threatened. As it was, growing up in captivity, he knew humans only through pain. His need to avoid them was great or perhaps he would have wandered close to towns, sniffing out bins for scraps of food which were more familiar to him than spawning salmon or sweet berries in the wild. Now, winter had withdrawn all the earth's nourishment and food was hard to come by. His body weakened while he searched and found little to sustain it.

But he also knew humans to be his only reliable source of food when he had none to protect. They had taught him that if he wanted food, he should amuse them. He should wave his paw, he should mimic them and hold at bay all his instincts to avoid them. It was essential for this bear to have the security of a source of food. And his instinct drew him closer to the only human who brought him food without hurting him, without asking for anything in return.

CHAPTER FIFTEEN

The bear was easy to find without looking. The moment I saw him coming in the distance of the woods and the wilds, my heart popped. All my grievances vanished at the immensity of this beautiful brown bear. He was astonishingly alive in the cold winter stillness, slowing as he came closer. I hadn't expected him to react so quickly to seeing me. My heart raced as the distance between us closed.

He hesitated several paces away to look at me

and I couldn't help but marvel at him. I believed he wanted me there, whatever the mysterious reason. But as I took a tentative step towards him, I lost sight of where my feet were treading. I tripped on roots below the snow and landed face down. Snow was up my nose, in my ears, under my collar. When I looked up, Bear was within bear-arm's reach.

His great jaws opened wide and I could see right inside to his pink tongue and the ribbed roof of his mouth, his jaws half empty, half full of curved and broken dark yellow teeth.

'No, no, no,' I said breathlessly, so as not to startle him. 'I've got a pie. Eat the pie instead.'

I pushed out my arm and made the same halt sign I had in the beginning. But Bear only yawned. He did not have whiskers. His eyes were walnut brown. His nose quivered but he did not come closer.

'I know you must be hungry,' I said. 'But you are not to eat me. Understand?'

Bear took a couple of steps back and sat down as if

he was suddenly aware of his great size compared to mine. I pushed myself up on to my hands and knees and held his eyes for a moment. His expression was soft and sad, a frown between his eyes, as if I was to understand that he had only meant to smell what I had brought, that he was hungry but didn't want to hurt me.

'You weren't going to eat me, though, were you?'

Maybe he'd seen me fall and had come to rescue me. I imagined all sorts of things about the bear and what might be going on inside his broad head full of brains.

I had fallen on the pie and squashed it and could smell the sweet aroma of sticky berries from my satchel. Pastry crumbs and blueberry juice had seeped out of the wrapping and smeared purple on to the lip of my satchel. I realized this was what he wanted. I emptied the crumbs from my satchel and unwrapped what was left of the pie.

'It looked nicer earlier but it'll taste the same.

My mum often says that. She makes sausage rolls for Christmas. If she was here, she'd let you have some.' I liked talking to the bear. I liked what I could talk about with him. He seemed to like hearing me too and it kept him calm.

To the left of us I noticed a clearing; a deep pool of untouched snow. I left the pie, taking a small piece with me as it smelled so good, and then backed away to the clearing. Slowly Bear lumbered over to the pie and sat down. He seemed so happy, his ears rounded forwards, his frown gone, as he dug into the pie with his long claws. I stepped into the unbroken snow and watched Bear lick at the spilled blueberries on his fur, crunching into the pastry. I tasted the piece I'd kept too. I loved that we were sharing it.

'At home we have mince pies but this is good too,' I said, patting my tummy. Bear made a moaning kind of sound and then patted his own tummy. It was so extraordinary being with the bear that the thought of who was missing out on the pie floated out of my mind altogether. I felt sure by his behaviour that he was in some way used to people, although I had strong doubts that he had been cared for properly. Why else was he out here, hungry, underfed, so sad?

With the pie finished, Bear wanted to play. He threw himself at the snow like a digger truck, skidding into it and sending it flying, and it made me want to join in, although I was still careful to remain at a distance. I threw armfuls of snow that fell down on me again. In the middle of the clearing I made a snowman, with fir cone eyes and twig arms. I was caught up with the festive feeling, as if I was in a Christmas card landscape, unbelievably with a bear! He snuffled in the snow, tossing it up and showering his head. For a moment I couldn't have asked for anything more.

All that was left of Inge's blueberry pie was a smudge of purple on the snow. I'd have to go back to the house sooner or later and face the consequences of taking it. I didn't want to feel bad. Not when I had felt so good. I sat down and looked at my boots. I was warm in the coat. My feet were warm too and I hadn't felt the cold at all. I changed my mind about them. The boots were blue, so I supposed that was something as it was Henry's favourite colour. They had a thick lining of fake sheepskin (V would approve) that went up to the top and curled over the rim. They were waterproof, the soles were thick and my feet had been impervious to the bite of the cold. Most of all, they had brought me to the bear. They were not such a bad gift after all.

Bear lumbered over to the snowman. He wandered around it, sniffing and nudging with his nose, and then sat down beside it.

'They are going to be mad at me as anything when there's no pie,' I told him. I was glad that Bear had eaten the pie. But I knew I would be in trouble and that I was making things worse with

Henry's family because of my behaviour.

The woods and the wilds closed in with shadows as the sun dipped behind the mountains.

'I'm going to write about you.' Bear hung his head as I left, drooping beside the cold snowman. 'I'll come back tomorrow.' His eyes followed me as I kept turning to look at him, all alone. The hump on his shoulders seemed more pronounced.

I went to V's. She welcomed me, even though the shop was busy with customers. She asked how I was, saying how deep in thought I looked, how it excited her to see a writer at work. I barely noticed anything else as I sat there making notes and then writing with the typewriter on my lap, reliving special moments with the bear, turning it into the growing middle of my story.

On my way back, I met Elissa, scowling fiercely.

She did it so well she must have had plenty of practice.

'I've been looking all around town for you! You were not supposed to go for so long,' she said, barely hiding her irritation. 'Where have you been? Are you trying to get me in trouble for losing you?'

The wonder of my encounter with Bear in the woods far outshone the weight of the worry about the pie and I found myself simply revealing the empty pie dish to her.

Elissa was baffled. 'You went back ... Why would you take a pie out of the house?' She folded her arms. 'You ate the pie, didn't you? Why are you copying Lars?'

'Yes,' I told Elissa. 'It tasted delicious.'

Henry did not respond to my confession about the pie as I had hoped, although it was Elissa who reported to the family what I had done. Instead of being sympathetic as Henry had been with Lars, or disappointed which I should have expected, Henry seemed embarrassed by my behaviour. And I was embarrassed too, despite the fact that I felt silently justified in feeding the pie to the bear. I would never have done anything like this at home, but I suppose I was trying to make some kind of point about the fact that this family had taken what I believed to be mine – namely my connection to my father – and therefore my birthday and Christmas didn't have the shared family meaning I wanted them to.

Eventually, after Henry and Inge had a quiet talk out of earshot, Henry told me, 'I'll finish work early tomorrow. We can do something together.'

So you could say there was a good outcome to it all. Henry was going to spend some time with me. I didn't try to plan what we might do together. All my plotting so far bore no resemblance to how things had turned out.

CHAPTER SIXTEEN

On that fourth day of my holiday, Lars had been left with me for the morning until Henry came home later that afternoon. Once again there was no mention of putting up decorations or getting a Christmas tree. I wanted to visit the bear again but with Lars lurking about I had no chance to pilfer any food. I decided to go to town first to buy something. I told Lars that I wanted to go on my own to do some Christmas shopping. It seemed like the best excuse to stop him tailing me.

'What have you got in your satchel?' he asked.

'Nothing!' I suppose he had only been checking to see if I'd stolen any food. I had nothing to hide but was spiky with the accusation.

'Inge said we have to ask if we are hungry,' he said.

There wasn't a sentence that passed his lips that didn't make me bristle. '*My dad* didn't say that.' I chose my words purposefully, fuelled by the unwelcome sense of the other family and their way of doing things. 'And anyway, I wouldn't want the lousy meatballs.'

'My mother made the lousy meatballs,' Lars said, though without malice.

Enraged, even though Lars was only stating facts, I told him it was the worst Christmas I had ever had. It occurred to me briefly, as I stormed off into town, that I might have been glad of Lars's company if I thought he had nothing to do with taking Henry away from me.

With my head in a messy place I found myself at

V's door. I trudged into the shop before taking up my normal spot at the top of the stepladder with the typewriter on my lap. My movements caused the ceiling decorations to twirl and the lights reflected like magic glitter.

I rolled a new piece of paper in the typewriter and I found myself writing about the horrible feelings I had towards Henry for going off with Lars and how Lars seemed to be able to share something with him that I did not. It helped a little to describe Henry in the worst possible way, to see if it felt true when I read it back on paper. But it was all so shallow and meaningless compared to the awe and wonderment I felt with the bear. When I came to show Henry my story, I'd leave those pages about him out. They were only meant for sorting out my thoughts, getting the bad feelings off my chest, but for now I had nothing else to write about him.

'How's the story going, Thea Whittington?' V was cleaning with a feather duster, rearranging lampshades and top hats between the tinsel and fairy lights. All the customers had gone. I looked round and did a double-take, having hardly noticed V when I'd come in, distracted by my thoughts. She wore a tweed suit, with wide-legged trousers and a strawberry-coloured beret. Her hair was shorter, black, smooth and straight around her face. I wasn't sure if this was her hair and the longer brown hair was a wig.

'Something up?' she said.

'No.' I sighed. 'Maybe.' I watched her for a moment. I thought it might be rude to point out that she looked like a completely different person. She seemed to be in a theatre or show of her own; her movements almost choreographed. Although I was her only audience, I assumed she was like this even when she was by herself, in her own invented drama productions, or some stories that she kept to herself inspired by all the vintage objects around her. She must have guessed by my stare what I was wondering.

'These were my mother's clothes,' she said. 'You know I miss her.' She reached up to spin some baubles on the chandeliers. 'We made these together a long, long time ago.'

It was an even better explanation than I had anticipated. V's ingenuity had created a rare connection with her mother which I had yet to find with Henry.

'When did you start putting your decorations up?' I asked.

'First day of December. You?'

'At home we put them up on the tenth of December, the day before my birthday . . .' I told her about my mum, home, and that I was here staying with Henry and his new family and how I felt I was missing this important part of the year because I couldn't share it with my father. 'I wanted to write about being with him, but at the moment he's not in my story how I wanted him to be.'

'It must be challenging being a writer.' She

twirled, unbuttoned her jacket and slipped out of the sleeves, putting it over a chair, resting her hands on the jacket shoulders as if her mother was still in it. 'And there will be many more challenges in your life, Thea Whittington. We all have to find out who matters and how to bring ourselves close to them.'

I liked her so much and she gave me hope that there would be a way back to Henry through sharing the story that I was writing, even though it wasn't yet quite what I wanted to show him.

The objects in the shop had become familiar over the last couple of days. I wandered around, touching things. I could almost feel them come alive, their stories, the people who had owned them seeping out and into the spaces between. I touched boots where someone's toes had once worn their own particular shape into the leather, the shimmering beads on an evening gown. I picked up the teddy bear again, readjusted his position, straightened the bow, and in that plumping of the ribbon and straightening of his back I felt that anything could mean something to another person when they opened their heart to it. In noticing all these things, and sharing the space in the shop with them, a kind of confidence grew in me that all I had to do was to continue to write things as I saw them. It would be enough for now. I still had a lot to learn about being a writer. I sat back down and carried on writing about everything I had seen so far, like a diary – V, the shop, Lars, Henry, but most of all about me and the bear.

Someone came into the shop. V looked over and in Norwegian greeted an older woman bundled in a yellow padded coat. Back with the typewriter in my lap, honest words continued to flow through to my fingers while the woman had a long conversation with V, whose hands were gracefully slipped inside the trouser pockets, thumbs with strawberry nails hooked outside.

After the customer had left, V was quiet, sitting on a chair, licking strips of gold and silver paper to make paper chains, a delicate frown between her pencilled eyebrows, while I typed what had happened yesterday.

'You know, Thea dearest, I've had three conversations in two days with people who came in here, all about the same subject,' she said. 'Bears.'

The hairs prickled on my scalp and I looked up.

'The woman who was in my shop was called Miss Anders and she told me she was looking for an escaped bear.' Her eyes flicked up to me then away again. 'She has been trying to track one that escaped in Russia months ago. And beastly Mr Prag was also looking for a bear in the woods. A *real* bear,' she stressed. 'It's extremely unusual to come across one around here, let alone two. There are some bears much further north of here near the borders with Russia, Sweden and Finland, but there are not so many as there used to be.' She squinted, paused and then sighed. 'I wonder if it is actually the same bear they are looking for.'

I still thought it best not to declare my interest in the bear. I shrugged, trying to make light of it. 'And who else was talking to you about bears?'

'You, of course.' She looked down again at the paper chains in her lap. 'It's quite a coincidence, don't you think, that you were asking about bears and you came back from the woods looking rather shaken?'

'Mm.' I nodded, lips curled inwards. 'It is a coincidence, isn't it?'

'Unfortunately, Mr Prag is awfully alarmed and wants everyone in town to know that one might be close by. He's a terrible worrywart.'

Then V asked me to help hang the strings of paper chains across the ceiling. Even though I liked her immensely, I thought that she might worry too, perhaps even stop me from seeing the bear again. I had only known V for a few days but I guessed her loyalties were most likely with the people of the town, even if that included the unlikeable Mr Prag. I didn't like the thought of him finding my bear.

'What will happen if they find the bear?' I asked.

'That will depend on who finds it first.'

I didn't want to sound too interested but I would have very much liked a fuller answer to my question. What would they do? If anyone else knew where he was, they might want to see him too and wouldn't that scare him away? Or if they captured him and took him away then I'd miss out on what felt like the most amazing privilege I'd ever had. I convinced myself the bear couldn't be the one Mr Prag was looking for, because any sense of alarm didn't match up to my experience of the gentle, almost-human bear that I'd encountered. An escaped bear? I chose not to think so. I said nothing, though I had an uncomfortable niggle in my stomach. V shrugged and held out some paper strips to me.

'Do you want some of these to make your bedroom more like Christmas?'

She gave me some to take back to the house, and as I left, said, 'Stay safe, Thea Whittington, and if you see a bear, you be sure to tell someone.'

I nodded.

'Promise me.'

I stuffed the paper chains in my satchel and told V that I would. I wasn't lying, I told myself. I *would* tell V about the bear but only at the end of my stay. Maybe it was selfish but I couldn't help wanting just a bit more time with him, just the two of us with our special connection, before he was discovered. At the end of my stay I would tell V about the bear and explain how wonderful, how human and gentle he was, and hand over the responsibility to her.

CHAPTER SEVENTEEN

I thought only of the good bear and me. I dismissed thoughts of the few days I had left with him while I was in Norway and how hard it might be to leave him. The desire to spend time with him was urgent and strong. Knowing that other people were looking for him, people who might want to hurt him even or take him away, made me want to look after him and keep him to myself all the more.

I stopped at the fruit and veg shop on the way to

see him and bought as many punnets of blueberries as they had (which wasn't many) and six packets of honey wafer-biscuits. It left me short of money for Christmas presents, but I hadn't been feeling very generous towards Henry or his family anyway.

I found the bear where I'd seen him before, as if this was now our agreed meeting place, where we knew to find each other. I no longer felt scared and was overwhelmed with joy at seeing him. He looked as if he had been patiently waiting for me and followed me at a distance as we explored deeper into the forest. I ran ahead, jumping up to hide wafers in the branches of trees and let him find them. Bear rose to his full magnificent height to take the biscuits, then sat down and ate each one slowly and deliberately, chewing on one side where there were more teeth. My heart blossomed just watching him.

I looked back as I high-stepped through drifts, Bear looking down to sniff at the foot-holes I made in the snow, crushing my steps and overpowering them with his. Deeper and further into the forest we went until I felt we were far out of everyone's way.

As we walked, I couldn't help looking up. The trees soared in their thick snow coats. We came across a particularly tall spruce tree, hung with long thin pine cones.

I wanted to share the view and I thought of Mum, how we'd invite each other to share the things we loved. It seemed right that Bear be part of what I felt too.

'Imagine having this as your Christmas tree, Bear,' I told him. The tree trunk was huge, and with a surge of joy I wrapped my arms around it. I lay my warmed cheek against it for a whole minute.

Although I moved away and meant to continue on, Bear stopped to inspect the tree too. He walked all the way around, his nose seeming to drink in a scent, before he planted his great behind down and leaned his back against it.

Bear wriggled against the tree. Everything about him touched and filled me. I began to imagine the tree ablaze with lights, the fine scales of the cigar-like cones even more golden. Those I loved around it, gazing up to the top with the halo of blue sky around it. I leaned back to look to where it was impossible to put a star but perfectly possible to invent one. Bear looked up too.

Being with Bear made me forget everything else. His paws dangled in the air, his hips hesitantly swayed as he grunted and groaned, scratching his back against the scaly bark. I could hardly believe my good fortune at seeing a smile curve into his lips as his eyes half closed with the pleasure of scratching. There was nothing but the magic of the glorious bear.

Bear danced out some long-held itch, even though his joints seemed stiff. The pleasure of seeing him ease a little in his great bear body made me want to sing, and what with it being close to Christmas, I felt a carol would be appropriate. I sang 'Good

King Wenceslas'. It had snow in the first couple of lines, although I couldn't remember all the words. At the sound of my singing Bear slid down the tree and sat in the snow, gazing at me at first, and then he looked off into the distance, his nose raised, sniffing at the air. Was he remembering something? When I finished the carol, he looked at me expectantly as if waiting for me to sing again. I sang him another carol and then wanted to dance. He didn't look away again. What kind of life had he had that he cared so much to give my voice and movement all his interest? And I had so missed being free and myself like this when I was with Henry and his family. The intense mixture of happiness and sadness in the bear's eyes as he watched is not one I have found a word to describe. I so wanted to take the sadness away.

'What do you think about making this tree *our* Christmas tree?' I said.

I declared the giant spruce suitable for our

purpose. I had the paper chains in my satchel and licked and stuck them together. I took a paper chain over to the edges of the spread of the tree, jumping up to drape it over the branches. Bear came towards me, slowly, a careful step at a time, his head low, swaying a little. He seemed anxious, even afraid, but perhaps his curiosity for the tree branches and what was in them kept him coming.

He raised his nose to sniff at the garlands, the frown on his forehead easing as he stood there quietly. I didn't think, I took off my glove, reached out and stroked him. He leaned into my hand a little, just enough for my fingers to melt into his fur, and I remembered how only a few days ago I had thought I would die having found myself so close. The thrill of touching him, the warmth of that physical meeting, that closeness bubbled and bubbled inside me.

'This is what Christmas is like,' I told him. 'Isn't it lovely?'

A memory of Henry holding me up when I was little filled my mind, briefly, the fullness of the feeling expanding before fading again. I saw something of what I'd felt all those years ago in Bear's eyes when he turned towards me, as if this small, simple thing of looking up into a Christmas tree with someone you loved was everything. My fingers itched to write, to find a way to tell something of this.

Bear suddenly jumped away from me, flattening himself down to the ground. He panted, looking around as if he was about to get caught, his nose up, his ears back, crawling like a beaten dog and so unlike a bear, towards the shadows of a thicket of trees. I heard it too, the distant voices of a small group of people, and stayed low, heading to hide behind our tree trunk. Bear's eyes were wildly afraid and he seemed unsure. Although I didn't want us to be seen, Bear's fear of being found seemed much greater than mine.

'They're not coming this way,' I whispered to him, although his sudden movement and the fear of being discovered made my blood rush. 'Come on, let's go this way. Stay with me.'

I walked away, staying low, not hurrying too much so as not to alarm him. He followed, passing me quickly as if monsters were after us.

I led the bear back towards his cave. I thought he ought to stay out of sight in case anyone else came this way. Then I crouched down to watch while he ambled into the shadows.

'You could probably do with a nap anyway. And I've got to see my dad.' I had a moment of longing that Henry wanted to share with me something of the magic I felt in the woods and the wilds.

I made a pile of the last of the biscuits and the blueberries. 'Please don't go back to sleep for the winter just yet. If you stay here, you'll be safe until I come back.'

Bear suddenly seemed anxious again, staring out

beyond me. I backed away, saying soothing things. When I turned round, my breath caught. Lars was standing at a short distance, staring through the trees. He stepped deliberately, placing his boots where mine had been, then following with his eyes the rest of the trail that led to me and the bear.

I strode towards him, my heart thumping. I was furious that he had been spying on me again, but more alarmed that he might have seen me with the bear and this would bring an end to my wonderful adventure. Lars turned and walked away before I got there.

'Lars! Come back!' He didn't wait and I had to run to catch him up. 'Why were you following me?'

'Henry is home, he sent me to find you.'

I had to do something, knowing I had no choice but to try and get him on my side after being so moody with him earlier. 'I've been meaning to say something.'

Lars marched on, head down, while I struggled

to think of what I could say to make him want to be friendly now, as I had either been short-tempered or avoided him so far. 'Sorry for what I said about the meatballs. I've never even tried a meatball so I don't know if they are lousy or not.' I squirmed at how pathetic it sounded. He plunged on through the snow, spaghetti hair bouncing out from under his hat.

'These are really good boots,' I said, as we got to the road. All I could do was carry on talking and hope I said something of interest to him. 'I didn't think so at first but my feet have stayed dry and warm. It must be because they are Norwegian.'

He glanced down at my boots and then back at me. He started walking faster so I grabbed his sleeve and with a little tartness on my tongue said, 'Don't you dare tell Dad where I was.' I remember calling Henry 'Dad' then, as if he was both ours, hoping that would give me some common ground to persuade Lars.

'He's not *my* dad,' he said and shrugged off my hand.

As I watched him walk ahead, I couldn't be sure if he'd seen the bear or not. The magical spell that bound me and the bear together felt as if it might be about to unravel.

CHAPTER EIGHTEEN

L ars didn't say another word on the way back to the house.

When we got to the workshop, he slipped past me through the door to where Henry was waiting for us.

The workshop smelled of Henry and Henry smelled of sawdust.

'I could show you how to make something out of wood,' Henry said casually, without a welcome or greeting. After the aliveness of the bear, Henry was like a piece of wood. He didn't even ask me if I wanted to do it. The tightness that had begun on seeing Lars squeezed my insides even more.

'Lars has got his own project but you can choose what you want to make,' he said.

It wasn't exactly sharing quality time; more like me being there while Henry did what he always did.

Lars walked straight past us without saying anything, briefly looking up at Henry, as I watched him warily, twitching with nerves in case he spilled the beans.

Henry was still finishing the sledge for a friend's family who had huskies, but there were other ongoing projects in the workshop, some abandoned, some waiting for repairs or half-finished. Wooden objects lay on benches and shelves, and hung from the rack above our heads. Curled shavings softened the floor. I hadn't taken much notice of what was in the workshop but I

imagined it to be like the inside of Henry's mind —
full of trees and bits of wood. I didn't think I had
a place in there.

I reminded myself that this was my first
opportunity to spend time with Henry, though
it was difficult to concentrate when so much else
was going on.

Lars settled himself on a stool with his chunk of
wood clamped in a vice on the bench and began
cutting at it with a chisel and hammer. It was the
same lump of wood he'd had the last few days,
although now more angular, as if it had elbows and
a rough idea of what it might be.

'What do you want to make?' Henry asked. He
shoved his hands in his pockets. 'A cup coaster,
a bookend, a walking stick? They're all easy.' He
seemed uncomfortable. I had been hoping for a
prompt to introduce the idea of the typewriter
again, perhaps mention the one in V's shop, but
I couldn't imagine making anything out of wood

that related to writing. I had learned something valuable from Bear though. I had understood what he needed first, which was the food. It had been a game, easy and fun when I'd hidden the salmon and left Bear to search. And from then he'd wanted to be with me. Maybe I needed to show some appreciation of Henry and his passion before trying to gain his interest in me or mine.

'I'd like to make some Christmas decorations. Little Christmas trees.'

On Henry's instruction I drew a template on paper for a little wooden Christmas tree. Rather than working with me, Henry dipped in and out to show me things but was deeply engrossed with working on finishing the sledge. I wanted to stay close to him, to show him I cared what I was doing like he did, and also to keep between him and Lars to avoid them talking. Henry barely looked up when I hovered nearby asking what I had to do next, but pointed to some thin wood, eventually laying down his tools for a short while to show me how to trace the design and cut it out using a small mechanical hacksaw with a fine-toothed blade.

I kept Lars in view out of the corner of my eye and was about to ask Henry for help making holes for the string to hang the ornaments when three men appeared, hailing Henry from the driveway, and he went out to meet them. One of them was Mr Prag. He was younger than the other men and yet undoubtedly the one in charge. His ear-flaps were tied under his chin this time; his hair sweaty, boots caked with ice. My mind raced. Was he here to tell Henry about the bear?

The men gathered together talking and Lars slipped off his stool, watching through the open door. In a panic, I drew him away from the doorway saying I needed his help to show me how to make a hole using a drill. The high pitch of the drilling drowned the men out for a moment and Lars gave nothing else away while he concentrated on holding the tool upright and steady. He turned the drill off and showed me how to sand around the hole to make it smooth. But not knowing if Lars was about to spring something to Henry and Mr Prag about me, or about me *and* the bear, I had to find out.

Lars suddenly said, 'Do you want to know what the men are saying to Henry?'

I hesitated, still unsure of Lars and his intentions. 'Is it about a bear?'

Lars nodded. Still no clue. 'The man in the red hat is Mr Prag. He's a town councillor—'

'I know who he is,' I said, a bit too snappily. I almost told him about V but didn't want Lars to know any of the places I went to avoid him. 'I've heard of him.'

'Oh,' he said, while my eyes narrowed with agonized impatience. 'Well, he's making sure everyone knows he's looking for a bear because he thinks it might be somewhere near here. He asked Henry if he's seen any tracks.'

My heart thumped wildly. 'And what did Henry say?'

'He hasn't seen a bear or tracks. But you have.'

Oh.

'Please don't say anything, Lars.'

'Why shouldn't I?'

I was thinking on my feet. 'I could tell you all about the bear . . . he's not like you think he would be,' I whispered. 'Please don't say anything, Lars. It's really important you don't. You'll soon see why, *if* you can keep secrets.'

His eyes widened, he whispered back, his natural eagerness immediately springing to life. 'Like what? Is it exciting?'

'Amazing . . .' I said, stalling, trying to work out how I could tell Lars and then not have him involved. 'But I'll have to tell you later.'

Lars put down his wood and stood up, turning towards the door. I grabbed his sleeve. 'I promise I'll tell you but not while they are here. It has to stay a secret between us.' I held his eyes with sheer determination. 'You have to check what else they are saying first.'

'Okay,' he said finally.

He listened in. 'Mr Prag is warning everyone to keep their eyes open because the bear will be hungry and it might head to town looking for food. He says the bear might even come here as we're the first house close to the woods.'

Lars twinkled with the idea of a secret between us. 'Are you trying to get the bear to come here? Is that the secret?'

I wanted the opposite. 'Not if I can help it.'

CHAPTER NINETEEN

Bear had come to mean so much to me, even in such a short space of time. He had brought light to my miserable heart, joy when I was down.

For the rest of the day I stalled Lars with excuses that Inge might hear or Henry might come back any moment. I needed a chance to think. I didn't know how far I could trust Lars or for how long.

At dinner that evening I took the seat at the table Inge now left for me next to Henry, who talked to the family about the possibility of a bear being nearby. Lars made saucer eyes at me. I ducked my chin down.

'That's strange,' Lars said, spearing a meatball and, with his elbow on the table, waving it about like a red flag. 'We've never seen a bear here before. Who actually saw it?'

'I'm not sure anyone has. Maybe someone saw tracks,' Henry said. 'Have you seen something?'

The silence while we waited for Lars to take a bite from the meatball, chew it slowly and swallow, was painful. 'I heard something,' he said.

'Who from?'

Lars stared across the table at me. I gritted my teeth and pierced him with my eyes, every muscle taut. 'Nobody,' he said, feeling the burn of my stare. 'Only Mr Prag earlier. I heard him talking to you.'

Thankfully Elissa interrupted Lars's charade, saying she'd seen Mr Prag in the café but he hadn't spoken to her and her friends. Inge said he wasn't good with children. I kept my head down and ate the meatballs, which, with gravy, were nicer than they looked.

'Nobody is to go to the woods until we know for sure.' Henry spoke to all of us in the same gruff, plain manner, with no special rules for me. I felt relieved in the knowledge that, so far, nobody but Lars had any idea I'd seen the bear.

'There's a meeting about it at seven thirty in town. I'll find out what Prag wants to do,' Henry said.

That caught my attention. I needed to know what would be said in the meeting. I was hoping to go with Henry, but afraid to ask and be rejected. What I needed was an ally and someone to translate for me without giving away my interest. There was only one obvious choice, although there was still only a shaky link and a promise between Lars and me.

I volunteered to help Lars clear the table while Inge and Elissa settled with some knitting and Henry built up the fire before he had to leave.

They didn't have a television and the whole family seemed to fill their time making things.

'I'm sorry you got in trouble about the salmon,' I quietly said to Lars, while I dried the kitchen utensils that he had washed. I smiled to show him I wasn't hugely annoyed or irritated by him, and using all my powers of persuasion, said, 'That's also part of the secret. I'll tell you about that later, but first, if you really want to be in on this—'

Lars interrupted. 'I think you gave the bear the salmon and the pie.' He seemed pleased at his own deductions.

I shushed him, checking to see if anyone was looking over. I lowered my voice further. 'There's a lot to tell you, but it's going to have to wait. First we're going to have to . . . to work together.'

'What do we have to do?' He looked suspicious.

'We need to get into that meeting with Henry and then you could translate what they say.'

'What's our cover story?'

'What?'

'We need a cover story if it's going to be secret.'

I rolled my eyes although half my heart was impressed at his thinking. 'Say you're helping me write a report or something. Maybe for school.'

'Do you like writing?'

The question stabbed at my heart. Not only had Henry ignored my request for the typewriter, he hadn't even shared what he should have known about me with his other family.

I sighed. 'Yes, I do. I want to be a writer.' But I was becoming more anxious by the second as across the room Henry checked his watch, got up, put on his coat and boots and headed to the door.

'Can you ask Inge if we can go?' My heart was speeding up. 'Please, Lars!' I urged as the door closed behind Henry.

Lars jumped to it and checked with Inge, giving her our cover story. Inge said, 'Henry has already gone.'

'We can run,' I said, Lars agreeing.

'Well, quickly, then, and catch up with him,' Inge said. 'And make sure you come home with Henry afterwards, okay?'

Henry walked fast but it only took us a minute of running to catch up with him. He turned round when he heard us coming.

'Inge said it was okay,' Lars said, when Henry snapped a look at each of us as we ran to his side. 'Thea wants to write about it for a school project.' Lars grinned at me. We were in this together now, whether I liked it or not.

CHAPTER TWENTY

A warm light spread around the café where I'd been with Elissa, and where the meeting was being held after opening hours. The windows were steamed up, the room packed. We wriggled our way through elbows in thick jumpers to stand by Henry near the front. While we waited for everyone to arrive, I asked Lars to tell me a few Norwegian words to see if I could get the gist of some of the conversation. It was a great advantage to have most people speak

English, but I had no Norwegian language at all. I thought Henry should have taught me.

Lars only had time to teach me that yes was *ja*, no was *nei*, and bear was *bjørn* before Mr Prag came to the front and propped a large map of the area up on the serving counter for everyone to see. His presence brought the room to a hush and he began to speak.

Lars translated that Mr Prag knew for sure there was a bear about because he'd spoken with a Miss Anders who had been tracking it. He was sure the bear was in the area, although the route its tracks had taken was unclear. He said everyone should be aware that this bear was probably within a few miles' radius of their town and was a great threat to their community.

It had taken repeated visits, food and assurance before the bear had trusted me but I couldn't entirely be sure that he would be gentle with anyone else. I remembered he had been afraid when he'd heard voices in the woods and it felt so unfair that Mr Prag was stirring everyone up to think the worst.

Lars told me that Mr Prag really didn't like bears. He'd been chased by one when he was a boy.

'He nearly died, he says,' Lars added solemnly.

I imagined Mr Prag might have done something to deserve being chased by a bear but knew it was inappropriate to say that out loud.

Lars paused, then he whispered, '*You* don't look like you nearly died.'

'I think the bear trusts me,' I said. It was the first thoughtful thing I had said to Lars. It seemed enough for him for now and he went back to translating.

'Mr Prag wants people to come with him and make a search party.' I had a sudden, horrifying vision of Mr Prag leading an angry mob with nets and chains and sticks taking out their fear on the bear. I hated the thought of him being captured or hurt. Then V made an entrance into our conversation like a movie star demanding we look at her instead.

'Hello, Thea Whittington. May I have a word with you?' She smiled at Lars to excuse us. I told Lars I was relying on him to make sure he got all the information we needed before V led me over to a quieter corner. Her make-up was immaculate as usual, her hair (brown again today) was pulled back into a low bun under a trilby hat. She wore a long pale trench coat, tied tight at the waist, suede gloves, buttoned at the wrist, and her slender ankles in high heels stood out among all the pairs of thick warm boots.

'I am extremely fond of bears,' she said. 'Would I be right in saying that you have a thing about bears too, my darling?'

'Yes, I love bears.' I wondered where this was going. Did V know something?

V raised her fine eyebrows, unbuttoned her gloves and slipped them off. She reminded me of a spy. 'Because I need to know if you are on my side, *and* on the bear's side.'

'I am, I am!' I nodded, waiting to hear what else she had to say.

She asked if I had noticed the woman who had come into her shop, wearing a yellow coat. 'Her name is Miss Anders. Remember I told you she was looking for a bear?' She relayed what Miss Anders had told her about the bear: that it had been captured as a cub, used as entertainment, and for carrying arms; that the bear had been treated very badly and that Miss Anders belonged to a worldwide organization that intended to rescue it and take it to a sanctuary.

Bear's reactions, my questions about him all began to make sense now. No wonder he had been afraid, because of how he knew humans. My heart blossomed at the thought that I had been able to show him I was no threat *to him*, and that was why he had trusted me and I had been safe with him too.

'The bear's captors let him go when he became too old to dance for them,' V continued. I felt tears well in my eyes when I thought of how Bear had looked when I danced for him. 'It's heartbreaking, I know,' she said as I blinked the tears away and she rubbed at my shoulder.

'Anyway, since then, people have reported seeing the bear in Finland, Sweden and recently in Norway, not far from here. Miss Anders has been plotting the bear's tracks and reported sightings. She knows it must be around here somewhere.'

V leaned down. She recalled me returning shaken from the woods. 'I have a nose for things. And I am beginning to wonder if the story you have been writing about your holiday has a real bear in it.'

'Stories are a kind of mixture of make-believe . . .' I began to suggest, still unwilling to betray the bear, still unsure how I could protect him.

'I understand what a story is, Thea darling. But you must understand that Miss Anders might be a little worried about that old bear at the moment. And I am. If I'm right, I sense you might be too.' V twitched her scarlet, perfectly formed lips as she glanced over at Mr Prag. 'Have you seen tracks in the woods?'

V wanted to protect the bear too and I knew I had to at last admit something to her.

'I saw it.'

'You saw it!'

I flapped my hands to make her keep her voice down. The tension was growing inside me and in the atmosphere. I could feel Mr Prag's determination from across the room as he drew everyone in, heightening their fears.

'Actually, I met it, but please don't tell Mr Prag.'

V gasped and muttered something in Norwegian.

'Leaving the fact you *met* the bear aside for now, dear child, there is another very pressing matter. I have known Mr Prag since we were children, when he had his so-called encounter with a bear.

He was quite all right, not a mark on him in fact, and I suspect if he was chased, he may well have warranted being warned off. He's like a dog with a bone about bears. He won't give up and he's doing a good job of scaremongering everyone around to his way of thinking. Is there anything else you can tell me before that man does something stupid?'

'Maybe the bear has gone off somewhere quiet to hibernate now,' I said, stalling. I was undecided about what I should keep to myself and what, for the bear's sake, I needed to share.

'Thea!' V said, as she must have sensed I was withholding information. 'Do you know where the bear is?'

Lars peered around a pillar beside V but I suspected he'd been there longer, listening in. V recognized Lars, and he assured her that he was on the bear's side too.

'What if we tell Mr Prag to let Miss Anders find the bear first?' Lars said, confirming my suspicions.

'I doubt he'll listen,' V said.

'What else has he been saying, Lars?' I asked.

'He's divided up the area and is organizing search parties for the morning.'

I wanted more than anything for this not to be happening, to keep Bear from all of this. But it was too late for that. If they found him, he would be scared. I might never see him again. 'I'll tell Miss Anders where the bear is. We have to speak to her first,' I said, finally.

'Okay, darlings. I'll do what I can.' V straightened her back and strode over to Mr Prag. It had a decidedly bad effect on him. Someone else overheard V and another conversation soon arose while Henry pushed through the crowd to make his way over to them. Voices were raised again.

'Where are the search parties going?' I asked Lars.

'Lots of places! Everywhere!'

It hadn't worked. What V said only seemed to make Mr Prag more angry, talking over her. I didn't have time to think it through as my fears for Bear's safety overpowered everything. 'Lars, come with me! I need your help!'

I pushed through the crowd. I had to do something to distract them.

I climbed onto the counter and loudly said, 'I know where the bear is!'

CHAPTER TWENTY-ONE

The crowd in the café fell quiet. Lars made his way over and stood below me while I stood on top of the counter.

'Can you tell them what I say?'

Lars nodded. For the first time, I wondered if I might have misjudged him. He seemed to be on my side, or at least on the bear's side.

'You don't need to be afraid of the bear,' I said. A murmur rose as Lars conveyed my words to the older generation who didn't speak much English. I had a feeling I could calm them as I had calmed the bear. 'I know because I've seen him.'

People looked at each other, murmured again and then returned their attention to me. I could see V nodding, speaking quietly to someone beside her, Henry staring intently at me.

I carried on. 'I know he's a good bear—' Mr Prag suddenly caught me around the waist and lowered me down from the counter.

'Hey!' I said. 'I've got something to say!' but he ignored my indignance, pushing aside Lars who'd come to my aid.

Mr Prag pointed out where the town was on the map, Henry's house, the road out towards the forest where I had gone several times, with and without good boots. I looked to Henry now to help me but he remained stern and immobile.

'Where did you see the bear?' Mr Prag said.

I ignored the question and tried to continue with what I had been going to say. 'He is good, but he's scared of people. If we leave him alone and let Miss Anders find him, then everyone can be safe and so can he.' It made sense to me but I could see it wasn't what they wanted to hear. Besides, why would they believe me? I was a stranger to them, and I had hardly believed it myself at first. And they hadn't seen what I had with my own eyes.

Henry was making his way over to us now. Mr Prag leaned in and whispered something in his ear.

'Just tell us where you saw it,' Henry said. I was unnerved by the fact that I couldn't tell where Henry stood on the matter, with him there beside Mr Prag who I could not trust.

'I'll show you,' I said, holding my nerve for what I was about to do.

Nearby, V flashed her eyes at me and shook her head.

'There.' I pointed on the map.

V covered her eyes but Lars looked undisturbed by my revelation. He even smiled. And I had an inkling he was a lot smarter than I'd given him credit for because he'd guessed what I'd done. I only hoped nobody else did.

Mr Prag marked an X on the spot and drew a wide circle around it. Now that I had told them what they wanted to hear, nobody was interested in me or in anything else I had to say, and I was jostled out from the front. Hands and voices were raised while Henry stood quietly by, his eyes questioning. I wriggled away to seek out V.

'What have you done, Thea? You've led Mr Prag directly to the bear.'

'I wouldn't do that,' I whispered.

'I knew it,' Lars said, muscling his way in.

V's gaze lingered over me for a moment as she understood. She cupped her hands around her mouth to whisper. She smelled so sweet, like a florist, up close.

'Have you sent them on a wild goose chase, my darling?'

I nodded. 'Now all we have to do is tell Miss Anders.'

'She left me a phone number . . . I wanted her to be here.' V bit her lip. 'But I couldn't get through.'

'There are some telephone lines down, south of here,' Lars said. My heart sank like a stone at the news.

'Don't worry, I'll find another way to get in contact with her,' V said. 'You did well, dear Thea and Lars.' She handed me a small card with her shop phone number on it. 'If you hear anything that might be useful, then you must call me.' I slipped it into my pocket.

Henry stepped in. 'We're going home.' He ushered Lars and me away and towards the door, V following.

I turned back to whisper to V. 'Tell me as soon as you find her.'

She nodded, pulled the rim of her hat a little lower over her eyes, and slid on the gloves before carefully tottering off in her pointed heels. I had no choice but to go with Henry, although my heart wasn't with him at all. It was with the bear. I wanted to make sure nobody ever hurt him again. But the dread of what might happen if we didn't find Miss Anders had taken root in my heart.

Henry instructed Lars and me to walk either side of him on the way back to the house, shining his torch all around and far ahead in case a bear might be coming our way. I was suspicious of Mr Prag's closeness to Henry, but now that Mr Prag wasn't with us I wanted to properly explain to Henry. I thought I had a chance to get him on the bear's side too.

I talked fast to get it all out. I tried to judge his reaction by his expression but he wasn't giving anything away. '. . . and I made a Christmas tree for him and he loved it. It's just that he's scared of people because they have been so unkind to him but he's gentle and kind with me,' I finished.

Henry stopped in his tracks then, and turned to face me. 'The bear?'

'Yes, the bear! And so, you see, you just have to tell Mr Prag that when a bear is following you or standing up on his legs, which is a bit frightening at first but only because he is so big . . .' Henry marched on, shaking his head, and I had to trot to keep up '. . . but actually, he just doesn't want to get hurt.'

Henry seemed to have speeded up even more. 'The bear followed you?'

'Yes, it was a game.'

'Thea!' he snapped. 'Are you making this up?'

I was stunned for a moment. 'No, I'm telling you what happened.'

Henry shook his head again. 'Is this some silly story you're writing?' His words pierced my heart sharply. It was the first time he'd acknowledged my writing but only to dismiss it. I'd expected that he might be worried about me having been so close to a bear. I thought he would show some concern, hug me, anything to show that I meant something to him. I had even thought he might be proud that I had stood up for what I believed in. I hadn't anticipated that he wouldn't even believe me.

'I don't write silly stories!' I said, stung by his words. 'I write about things that are important and interesting to me.'

'This isn't a game,' he growled and stopped to face me. 'It's a serious situation!'

'And I'm very serious about helping the bear!'

'Stop with this nonsense!' he snapped, stinging me again, and I knew it was pointless to argue.

Henry rubbed at his face, then told us that if we saw a bear we were not to run, but to stand behind him. I felt further from Henry than I had when I was at home in Britain.

Henry had never been good at communicating. My mother often said he had been excitingly unknowable when she first met him, but when this wore off she had come to think of him as someone she would never be able to get close to. I understood much later in life how brave she had been to give up on Henry, to raise me by herself, to be a single woman again, but she'd always told me that having me with her gave her the strength to do what she knew she had to do.

A weight sunk into me, far heavier than the disappointment of not getting the typewriter. Couldn't something as enormous as a bear even bring us close? Was there really nothing that could connect us together?

Lars hung back to join me as I trudged slowly behind.

'*I* want to know everything about the bear,' he whispered. I should have heard what he meant. He offered to listen but I didn't answer, still wounded by thoughts of Henry.

'You know what they will do if they find the bear?' Lars said quietly, head hung, his eyes shielded by his crinkled fringe. I did not want to hear it. 'You know the bear that came into town once, the one that chased Mr Prag when he was a boy? His father shot it.'

I hadn't wanted to admit it to myself. Mr Prag was hunting the bear to kill him.

I lashed out at Lars for voicing what I feared the most. 'This is the worst place I have ever been, with the worst people I have ever met in my life!'

Even though the hunting parties might not be headed in the right direction, I didn't know how quickly they would cover the area or if they might widen their search or change course. And with Henry thinking I had made it all up, might he even discount where I had told them to look and try somewhere closer to home? Neither could I guarantee that the bear would stay put and out of sight. It all felt hopeless. At most, I had only hindered the search temporarily. I ran ahead, into the house, to Hess's room, shut the door and sobbed.

But I would never have given away where the bear was, not even if Henry offered me a brand spanking new electric typewriter and a litre of correcting fluid for all the mistakes I would make.

CHAPTER TWENTY-TWO

I t was the early hours of the twenty-third of December, my fifth day in Norway, and my heart had never been tested so much.

Henry's vigilance meant none of us children were allowed to leave the house on our own or without prior agreement or supervision. The plan was to mostly confine those who were not in the hunting parties to their homes too, or, if it was necessary to venture out, within a group that included at least two other brave adults. I wondered if Bear would be waiting for me to come with food. I lay awake thinking of the space between where I was and where he was in the woods. Would Bear attack the hunters if he saw them? Or would he be so afraid that he'd give up all hope of getting away?

Inge went off to work long before dawn and I was wide awake when I heard Henry leave to join the hunting party, even though it was barely light. I went downstairs. It struck me again how gloomy the house was. I missed finding Mum had got up earlier and turned on the Christmas lights to bring a glow to our house in the dark of a cold winter morning.

I was the only one awake and dressed and all I could think of was the bear. He was everything to me, the only good and bright place in my heart among all the shadows that Henry left. I needed to find a way to keep him hidden for as long as possible. My idea was to sneak out and make a larder in his cave until the search parties gave up.

I hoped it might only take a day or so, what with Christmas coming; Bear would go back to his cave and sleep, or Miss Anders would arrive to rescue him. I couldn't think further ahead.

I had seen Inge with large shopping bags over the last few days, presumably food for the Christmas period (although I had begun to doubt whether they celebrated with a Christmas lunch as even two days before Christmas there was still no sign that it was coming), but little of it had ended up in the kitchen cupboards. I searched everywhere but couldn't find where it was until I hit upon the idea that, as it was so cold, the food might have been stored somewhere outdoors. I kicked myself for not thinking of this before. Lars and Elissa's bedroom doors were still shut so I put on my coat, hat and boots, quietly unlocked the door and tiptoed around the side of the house. As I had thought, there were several cold boxes of supplies stacked in a space beside the log shelter.

I found a small pull-along sledge, which I assumed had belonged to Lars and Elissa when they were much younger, and strapped on melons, grapes, smoked salmon, bananas, cake and biscuits that I commandeered. Not stopping to speak to anyone, I towed the food to the woods as light began to thin the night into a navy dawn.

My heart expanded on seeing Bear pad towards me, his nose and ears high, almost as if he had called me to him and I, drawn by his presence, had to go. I wanted to tell him I loved him. I wanted to tell him how happy he made me; how glad I was that he was still safe. One way or another, time was running out for us. I wished I could hold on to this moment for ever.

I threw Bear a melon. He caught it, dropped it, and then tackled it like a rugby ball until he had it secured between his paws. He split the yellow skin and dug into the pulp and I saw in him the possibility of the wild, ferocious bear he could be if threatened by the hunters. That's why they were scared of him. They would not take the time to look into his eyes, to question and discover what he was really like.

'You were supposed to stay in your cave. I need you to do that,' I told him. 'I don't want Mr Prag finding you.'

Bear watched while I spoke, juice dribbling off his chin.

I struck upon the idea that I could disguise the cave. Even from a distance there were too many signs that might encourage someone to look here: the fallen branch had swept all the snow from the tree, the rockface had been exposed and there were a lot of footprints, both mine and the bear's. The shovel was still there and I began to dig at the mound of land-slipped snow, all the time watching the bear out of the corner of my eye. I could think of no better word to describe him than content, one moment digging into the food, the next watching me with even greater affection, free as he was from what was going on out of sight. I couldn't help picking at the grapes and biscuits as I'd not had breakfast, and it seemed to please Bear that I ate too. I kept on digging, working hard, piling the snow up like I'd seen along Henry's driveway. I formed a curve, shaping the snow which was the kind that builds the best snowmen, easily patted into solid objects. I moulded it into a wall, curving it inwards and around the corner of the rockface like half an igloo. Stepping back to see what it looked like from a distance, I made some alterations, banking up more and more snow until I could only just see over the top on tiptoe. The wall concealed the shadow of the entrance to Bear's cave and, if we were lucky, merely looked as if it was a drift of snow in front of a rock.

But no matter how much I moved snow around, our tracks had left many shadows and melted holes. I tried not to show him how worried I was but was becoming more and more desperate when I couldn't level it all out. Bear paced as if he sensed something was wrong and we ended up making more and more footprints.

'I'm sorry,' I told him. 'I only want to keep you safe, and it feels all wrong that you can't come out and we can't play and have our own kind of Christmas together.' I hated the thought that, one way or another, Bear would soon have to leave this place where he had found comfort after his long life of suffering. But I pushed everything aside until the sweetness and peace I felt with him was all that mattered.

I had only intended to stay for a short while, to make sure the bear remained hidden and had enough food, before trying to help contact Miss Anders. I lingered longer than I had meant to, singing

'Rudolph, the Red-Nosed Reindeer' because it was cheerful. Before I left, I stacked the rest of the food in Bear's cave.

'Now, you have to stay here and I know you will because you're a good bear. Beware of Mr Prag. He has a red hat and smells strong and fake like the perfume counter in a department store. You'll know him because you've met mean people like him before.' I hung my head. 'Be careful of a man wearing blue too.' It was the last thing I would have wanted to say.

'I'm sorry you've met people like this before,' I whispered. 'But I love you. And V does. Maybe Lars too.' But was it enough?

As I left, Bear poked his head out and over the top of the snow wall until I told him to go back inside the cave. My heart ached with how much he trusted me. I hoped I wouldn't let him down.

CHAPTER TWENTY-THREE

A light was on at the house. Elissa was in the sitting area in her pyjamas, the phone to her ear. I ducked to pass under the window, trying to think of an excuse. Being wide awake and alert, I noticed the empty log basket inside. I grabbed some logs from the pile and casually went in the front door.

Elissa turned as she heard me come in, her eyes flashing.

She muttered something and put the phone down. 'Where have you been?'

'I went outside to get some logs,' I said. I kept my cool although I had no idea how long Elissa had been up or known I'd been gone.

She narrowed her eyes, unconvinced. 'We're not supposed to go outside.'

'I was actually hoping someone could teach me how to light a fire.' I made it up on the spot, and fortunately Elissa seemed to relax when she noticed the empty log basket too.

'Lars will teach you,' she said, and huffed off upstairs. I heard her speak to Lars, then the bathroom door closed and the taps started running. She'd most likely be gone for ages. First possible disaster avoided.

'Elissa said you want to know how to light the fire,' Lars said, leaning over the banister on the landing upstairs. He was also still in his pyjamas so I guessed that both he and Elissa had only just got up, and perhaps Elissa had been on the phone to a friend (when she wasn't supposed to be) rather than alerting Henry or Inge that I was missing.

'Maybe later,' I said, as he jumped down the stairs. I really needed him for something else. 'Do you think we'd be allowed to make something in the workshop?'

'Like what?'

'Maybe you could help me with the idea too.'

'Okay. I'll get changed.' He galloped off back upstairs, pausing halfway up. 'If it's something to do with the bear, you can tell me.'

Could I trust Henry's blue-eyed would-be carpenter boy? A suspicion that he might have been asked by Henry to continue spying on me nibbled away at my trust.

As soon as he'd gone, I dialled V's number.

'I'm sorry, Thea, it's rather early and I still haven't been able to get hold of Miss Anders or find out where she is yet. I am trying.' She sighed heavily.

'Do you think Mr Prag might have told her there was no bear here?' It might suit his purpose for her to leave the area so he could hunt the bear for himself.

'I wouldn't put it past him,' V murmured.

'Do you know which hotel Miss Anders stayed at? She might have mentioned to them where she was going next.'

V had found the hotel she'd stayed at a few miles away but the phone lines were still down, and if Mr Prag had misdirected Miss Anders about where the bear was, she might even have left the area completely.

'I'm going to get in a taxi, darling, and drive around the hotels,' V said. 'I'll call you as soon as I find anything out. Have you any news about the bear?'

'He's sort of safe,' I said hesitantly. 'But I don't know for how long.'

In the meantime, I had to make sure that Mr

Prag kept looking in the wrong place. I called up the stairs for Lars to meet me in the workshop.

The workshop was full of objects expressed from Henry's ideas which I touched, held and thought about. I didn't know why I couldn't connect with them like he did.

I knew little about wood or what you could do with it. I didn't really have a particular plan but trusted inspiration might strike me at any moment with a way to keep the bear safe until V found Miss Anders. Maybe I could drag a plank of wood across the snow, possibly smoothing out the dips and dents of the footprints to disguise that Bear or I had ever been there? I took a good look at the sledge that Henry had been making. It was big enough for someone to ride on, with a long trailer about the length of a sleeping man. But even if I took it, I wasn't sure what I could do with it. Disguise the footprints with a sledge trail? Without a pack of huskies, it looked solid and too heavy for me to pull.

As soon as Lars appeared, bright and rosy-cheeked, I told him about the bear (although summarizing a lot), how I'd found him by accident, fed him salmon and pie just as Lars had guessed, but I concentrated on my mission as time was against us. I thought Lars deserved to hear about him after keeping his word about not telling Henry and translating at the meeting for me, but I wasn't prepared to answer him when he asked if I knew where the bear was now.

'It's more important that we stick together and keep quiet about it,' I said. Part of me couldn't be sure that Lars's bond with Henry wouldn't end up leading Mr Prag to the bear, and I had no intention of being careless over the bear's life.

'I'm not going to tell anyone where I saw you, not even Henry,' Lars said. I blinked at him a few times, but I remained cautious. 'What's the idea for the bear?' he continued.

'I want to make sure that the hunting parties don't go near him so I need something to disguise his tracks in the snow.'

Lars twitched his mouth for a moment and scanned the workshop.

'I know!' he said. 'Why don't we make bear tracks over the other side of town? We can make some fake ones. I'll show you how.'

Lars explained, collecting four thick slices of branch and drawing bear footprints on them. 'We can carve the wood away to leave the prints, stand on the blocks and then strap them over our boots, then when we walk we'll make bear footprints.' Lars said he had done something similar at school when he was younger, although they were deer prints. 'We need four blocks, because bears have four legs, and two people to make it work because we've only got two each. We'll have to do it together. It'll look more real.'

Between us we chiselled away the excess wood to reveal raised shapes of toes and claws with a heart-shaped pad in the middle. Lars nailed on webbing so we would be able to slip them over our boots like sandals. Hope swelled in my heart that we had a plan that might actually work.

Lars put them side by side. 'Oh. Two right feet.'

I sighed at the obvious mistake I had made, but Lars said that hopefully nobody would look too closely.

The door opened and Elissa appeared, arms folded. 'You two shouldn't have come out here. You know there's a wild bear on the loose!'

'The door was closed and we were safe until you opened it,' Lars said.

I couldn't help myself but I found Lars's wit funny, while acknowledging that Elissa must care. Elissa quickly stepped inside the workshop and closed the door behind her. She relaxed a little, asking to see what we'd made, but was uninterested when Lars held the blocks up and we offered no explanation. She probably thought they were table mats.

Elissa sat down on a stool, shuffling shavings with her toe. 'I'm so bored.'

The last thing I wanted now was Elissa delaying what was an urgent mission. Lars and I looked at each other and I communicated with my eyes and little flicks of my head that he should get rid of her quickly.

'Why don't you phone all your friends?' Lars said.

'You know we're only allowed to make phone calls in the evening,' Elissa said.

'If we're not allowed out, what else are we supposed to do? We'll go mad if we have to stay in the house by ourselves for days.'

Elissa took the bait. 'Good point. And it's the holidays too. Whether Henry likes it or not.' She glanced at me warily, as if I might react badly to what she'd said. I wasn't sure what she meant, only that I sensed as I had about the cooking Henry assumed she enjoyed that she found his lack of understanding of her difficult too. She headed for the door. 'Keep the door closed.' And off she ran back to the house to have what I imagined would be long telephone conversations with friends, phones crooked between ears and shoulders, listening to the clacking of each other's knitting needles.

Lars and I were ready to head out but I hesitated at the door.

'Thanks for . . . you know, with Elissa.' He had actually been brilliant. How had I not noticed this about him before? I was suddenly glad I wasn't doing this on my own.

'Do you know where to go?' Lars said.

I smiled. 'Could you show me?'

CHAPTER TWENTY-FOUR

We went into town, aiming to head out the other side, far from where the bear really was.

The town was deserted, so there was little risk of us being seen and someone calling Henry. Most of the shops were closed. I guessed shopkeepers must have joined the search parties or stayed at home. But the more people that were out looking, the quicker they would cover the ground and might head in a new direction.

Lars took me to a track leading to another area of the forest, smooth with snow, where nobody had been. We strapped the blocks to our boots and at first were merely trampling around, trying them out.

'We have to make this look convincing,' I said. 'The bear has four legs so . . .' I stood with my back to him, both of us in line. 'When I say right, step with your right foot—'

'No, the legs go like this,' he said, pointing out that a bear's back left foot would step after his front right foot.

'Oh, I see!' He was right.

But our feet were too far apart.

'We have to be like train carriages.' He made a train noise which made me laugh. I was grateful to him for keeping everything upbeat.

'Now, hold on to me,' I said. He put his arms around my waist but I wriggled out. 'Just hold my coat. The bear is very big so his legs are farther apart.' I heard him sigh. 'Now ready? My right, your left. Go!'

We made strides as best we could. When we stumbled or got out of sync Lars said even a bear could trip, and for a short while all we concentrated on was our joined-up walking. We made circles around an occasional tree (I told him more about what I had seen of the bear enjoying a scratch) and headed further and further, stamping bear tracks into the snow.

After a long while, I realized that I wasn't sure how we would get back without making the trail return to town or leaving our own footprints. Lars said we had to keep going until we came to a road. So we did. The road had been ploughed and scraped clear of snow and it made sense that the prints would end here. We took off the blocks, putting them inside my satchel, and walked a circular route on the road for miles and miles to get back. My energy was flagging but Lars must have been used to long walks.

As we came into town from a completely different direction, we heard many voices and the thud of boots about to come around the corner towards us. We dived into someone's front garden and hid behind a snow bank.

The hunting parties were returning to town. Had they found Bear? Was the search over? Lars grabbed me and tugged me back as the urge to run and find out was almost overwhelming. He shook his head and whispered, 'They're having a break, getting something to eat. It's okay.'

I felt relieved, and so weary all of a sudden. They'd soon be on their way again. Had we done enough to throw them off the scent?

We peered out to watch as they headed towards the café, knocking snow off their boots, peeling off coats and steaming up the windows as they gathered inside. Henry was with them.

'I need to go and see the bear,' I whispered. 'I have to make sure he stays hidden.'

Lars thought for a moment and I was sure he wanted to come with me, but he said, 'You go. I'll go and tell them I saw the bear prints where we've just been.'

I could have cried at his thoughtfulness. 'You're going to be in so much trouble for being out when we're not allowed.'

He shrugged. 'I'll work it out.' Lars's care and the thought of seeing the bear boosted my resolve. I kept my eye on the café, to see they had all gone inside and shut the door, before sneaking out from our hiding place. I kept low, but Lars got up, straightened his hat and marched towards the café while I hurried ahead. As I was looking back over my shoulder at Lars, I ran headfirst into Mr Prag. He had a rifle over his shoulder. Its cold glint shocked me.

I tried to run but he caught me by the hood of my coat.

He spoke to me in Norwegian at first.

'I'm going home,' I said, assuming what he might have said, trying to wriggle away at the same time.

'I remember you, little girl,' he said, speaking in English now. His eyes were pale and grey, probably like his heart; a narrow chimney of a heart that had never been on fire. 'Henry's niece?'

'Actually, I'm his daughter.' I circled around him so he'd change positions and so I could see what Lars was doing. He was entering the café now.

Mr Prag muttered something in Norwegian

again, before adding, 'There is no bear where you told us to look. No footprints. We're wasting our time. Henry told us it was a silly story.'

I smarted painfully at that. But could I use it to get Mr Prag to stop the search?

'Actually, he's right, I made it up. There isn't a bear,' I said.

'Ah, but, you see, I am sure there is.' He tapped his nose and narrowed his eyes, leaning his angular face towards me. 'Miss Anders showed me the map of its tracks and I know how bears think. It will be after food. It will come into our houses and eat little children like you unless I stop it.'

The harder he stared at me the more I thought of him as the wild predator. I stopped wriggling and pretended I was trying to help.

'Okay, maybe I made a mistake about where he is. I checked another map afterwards and I think I got it upside down. Try that way.' I pointed him in yet another direction. 'Now let go of me!'

I'm not sure I would have got away from his tight grip if the stupid brown coat hadn't been so big. I slipped out of it, grabbing my satchel as it slid off too, and ran. Mr Prag marched towards the café, calling out Henry's name, holding up my coat. I dived into the alleyway as Henry came outside with Lars and headed off to the woods. I needed to get to Bear and make sure he was okay.

I ran on, growing cold without the coat, uneasy that I hadn't convinced Mr Prag of much at all. Maybe Lars would do better than me. My legs were aching by the time I reached the woods. I had turned back every few seconds to see if I had been followed but nobody was there.

I didn't have to go far before I saw Bear, and my heart opened wide at the sight of him. He had come out of the cave and lay with his head on his chocolate coloured paws, surrounded by deep footprints in the snow that I knew were mine. It was worrying how easily I found him. The hunting party would have no trouble spotting him if they came this way. I realized in a rush that my footprints might lead them right to him. I had to hope Lars and I had succeeded in throwing them off the trail. As soon as Bear sensed me he raised his head, staggering up on to his four shaggy legs, a great lumbering monument of gentle wildness plodding his way to meet me. At a few metres from me he stopped, as if he sensed he needed to be in control of his own power. His nose quivered, his warm breath made white clouds in the cold air. He stood and watched me.

'Oh, Bear. You're supposed to stay in your cave.' Finding him I felt exhausted with all the miles I had covered, as if he was the destination at the end of a journey.

'I don't know how much time we have left,' I said. Whatever happened, I was going to lose this wonderful friend that I'd found.

Bear circled around me.

'Come on, we need to get you away from here.' I tried to go forward but he stood in front of me. I went around him and beckoned him to come. Again, he circled and stood in front of me as if he was trying to communicate something to me.

'We have to go, Bear. Please.'

But the bear just lay down in my path. I hesitated. Was he saying what I thought he was saying? Bear waited. I stepped closer and held the fur on his shoulders, pulled myself on to his back and swung my leg over. I lay forward, wrapping my arms around his neck, clinging to handfuls of fur. His coat was deep, bristly like sisal, so comfortingly strong, and I held on as if he was my safety harness. Every time he seemed to give me something more than I could give him.

Up he rose, standing still on four legs for a moment as if waiting to be sure I was secure.

'You can go slowly if I'm heavy,' I whispered, although I could hardly believe what was happening.

He carried me to the cave on the rough warmth of his back, and at the entrance he stood still to let me slide off. He went inside the cave, turned, his head poking out as he sat down.

As we faced each other, he looked at me with such care, and my heart collapsed almost as if I had drawn close enough to comfort to safely let the tears fall.

'I wish we were both at home with my mum.' I longed for her security, her warmth, to be curled up together on the sofa watching the tree twinkle. But no gift this year would have been greater than sharing Christmas with the bear. And in spite of the threat of Mr Prag and Henry's coldness, I felt peaceful here with him now.

As I put my hands up to wipe my eyes, Bear leaned in and licked them up, leaving a soft wetness on my cheek. He smacked his chops, swirling his giant pink tongue over his nose, and blinked at me tenderly. I believed more than anything he had tried to comfort me in the only way he knew how.

'Have you eaten everything I left you? I couldn't bring anything with me this time.' My teeth chattered. 'I'm sorry I don't have anything for you. And I'm sorry I'm crying, but horrible Mr Prag is scary because he's afraid of you.' I had never seen a gun before, and hoped to never see one again. 'I want to keep you safe. And I'm cold. And my dad isn't who I imagined he was. He's not your friend either.'

Bear watched me. His nose twitched. With my back against the rock, I slid down, wrapped my arms around my knees and rested my head.

CHAPTER TWENTY-FIVE

Before my eyes had opened, I knew I was warm but my nose told me I might be lying on a smelly old rug. I must have fallen asleep and slid over. I was still outside Bear's cave, hidden behind the snow wall, but Bear had moved over and I was now lying against him, curled into his shoulder. He was asleep. I didn't want to move from where I was sheltered. Gently I pushed my fingers into his fur, through the roughness of his outer protective coat, deep into the warmest finer hair. His heart beat powerfully and slow.

I'd never forget this moment. How lucky I was to have been cared for by a bear, one that might never have been cared for by anyone else. I'd write it all down, when I got the chance.

Bear stirred. His eyes opened but he didn't move.

It wasn't dark but I didn't know how long I'd slept.

I didn't hear any voices nearby but there was still much to do to ensure the bear's safety. 'I have to go,' I whispered. I knew his only chance was if Miss Anders got to him. Would this be the last time I saw him? My heart was breaking. But I didn't want him to know that anything was wrong. I wanted him to stay resting, peaceful and happy, like he deserved to be.

'You just carry on being a good bear.' He didn't want me to go and rose up and tried to follow.

'Stay here!' I commanded him, forcing myself to be firm. 'I'm sorry; I'm cross because I have to be and I don't mean it at all.'

I took off my hat and put it down on the ground between us. I thought perhaps it might smell of me, that I could leave it with him as a little piece of company. He dragged the hat towards himself with his claws and pinned it under his chin. He lay his head on his paw as I backed away, his eyes soft and pleading.

I trotted like a heavy pony through the woods and

the wilds, through the path of many deep bootprints that I'd left from my journeys to the bear.

I turned left at the edge of the woods and the wilds, and ran down the road. Henry was at the end of the drive, holding my coat.

CHAPTER TWENTY-SIX

Inge was already home after Elissa called her to say that Lars and I had gone missing.

'We have been very worried about you,' Inge said. It stung me that it wasn't Henry saying it. The amount of hurt that he was able to deliver without saying anything felt endless. He stood quietly by, face masked by his beard, heaviness around his eyes. Leaning against the kitchen counter, Elissa looked satisfied that I had finally proved what a horror I could be, although there was a kind of quiet relief about her that I had returned. Lars looked squashed, as if he might have had quite a telling-off, but he nodded to me as if to tell me we were still on the same side. A few days ago, I would not have thought I'd ever be glad to see him.

'Where have you been?' Henry said.

'I already told them you were looking for Miss Anders, Thea.' Lars looked at me meaningfully.

Henry squinted at us both. 'It's true,' I said, picking up on Lars's version of events. I didn't wait to be told off but offered only enough information that I thought would end what was about to be a soul-destroying interrogation. 'Nobody needs to find the bear except Miss Anders. The bear must have been hibernating and somebody woke him or something, I don't know. He was hungry, I expect, but he's probably gone back to sleep now. For the whole of winter.'

'There's food missing from the log store,' Inge said gravely.

Elissa was horrified. 'Maybe the bear came and ate it!'

Lars was quick to respond. 'There are no bear footprints outside. I looked around the house.'

'The bear won't hurt anyone and I don't want anyone to hurt the bear.' Frustration was getting the better of me. 'Why won't anyone listen to me?'

'She's writing a story about a bear,' Lars said. Henry sighed, as if still in disbelief about my writing, but it was enough to end the questioning.

Henry said something in Norwegian to Inge. She took Elissa by the arm and they went upstairs together, collecting Lars on the way, leaving Henry and me. At last I had Henry to myself, though not in the circumstances that I had wished for.

He paced a little, hands in pockets. 'It was too big a pie for one person,' he said.

'It wasn't too big. I told you in my letter, I've grown.' I was getting short on excuses and Henry's frustration with me was quick to show.

'You saw the bear.'

'Yes! I told you.'

'Did you take food for it?'

'He was hungry! If everyone looks for Miss Anders instead of the bear, then . . .' I trailed off, exhausted with trying. No matter what I said, he was not hearing me.

Out of the corner of my eye, I saw Lars's baggy socks near the top of the stairs. He must have crept down and was spying again. And although this time I was glad of his allegiance, it only made the hurt greater that I didn't have it from Henry.

Henry called out to Inge, who immediately came downstairs. 'Make sure Thea and Lars stay in the house this time.' He headed for the door.

I went after him as he picked up his van keys. 'Where are you going?'

'I'm supposed to be helping with the search.'

He accepted now that I had seen the bear and he had seen me come down the road from the woods.

I had given away the direction that would lead him to the bear's cave. Was he going to find Mr Prag and tell him?

'There's no need to hurt him!'

Henry's face was dark. 'If the bear thinks it will get food from humans, then someone might get hurt!'

'Just give us some more time!' I ran to the door but Inge was already there and stood between me and my way out.

'Thea, they have to make sure everyone is safe.'

'But the bear isn't safe!' While Inge was distracted with me, Lars slipped out behind her. I saw him through the window as he caught up with Henry. Henry opened the van window and pointed back to the house but stopped for half a minute while Lars spoke to him.

Henry drove off in the opposite direction to the woods and the wilds. To find Mr Prag and the hunting party first? I was overwhelmed with fear and fury. When Lars came back in he looked ashamed, avoiding my eyes. What had he done? Had he been playing me all along to get information to give to Henry? I didn't want to believe that but my mind was racing furiously. I wanted to kick him for being able to get to Henry when I couldn't.

Inge must have seen my frustration, the angry tears welling in my eyes. She put her hand on my shoulder.

'You have to stay here, Thea. You have to leave these matters to the adults now. Come on, it's nearly Christmas.'

'It doesn't feel like it.'

'Well, let's do something for Christmas.' Her cool patience calmed me slightly. 'It will help keep your mind occupied. Come on, Thea, come and help me.'

All my faith was in V now. I hoped it would turn out to be true that V would stand for victory.

Inge encouraged me to the kitchen where she lay

herrings in a tray and asked me to help her cover them in salt. They would be bottled tomorrow and eaten over Christmas. Inge told me about their family traditions, most of which they saved for Christmas Eve. Together they would go to the woods in the morning to choose a tree, chop it down and bring it into the house. They'd collect some sprigs from the woods to decorate the fireplace and table, and, in the evening, give their gifts to each other before they went to bed. I remembered V and her teacups and how, at first, I'd thought they were used and broken, until she told me what they meant to her. The traditions Mum and I had at home were different, but of course they had the same kind of meaning. And then I wondered: did it matter how anyone celebrated Christmas, as long as you shared it with someone? If it brought you close to them? If you continued over time to remember each year, didn't that make your traditions and connections stronger? It was the first time I stopped to notice how Inge, in her own way, had tried to be kind, had asked her children to spend time with me. I missed Mum so much at that moment. But although my journey had pushed Henry and me further apart, I did not for a second regret those treasured moments I had shared with the bear.

'We usually make each other something for Christmas,' Inge said. 'Henry and I will not be working tomorrow and we'll all be at home hurrying to finish our gifts.'

I realized then, that all this time, when I had been complaining about their lack of Christmas spirit, Elissa and her friends, and Inge, had been knitting Christmas gifts, Lars and Henry making gifts from wood. I had not noticed the Christmas they were already having. At home, the proof of Christmas spirit was in the decorations, the lights, the sausage rolls and gingerbread, and the gift-wrapped presents under the tree. Being with the one I loved. I hadn't recognized what it meant to them.

'And you made something with your father, didn't you?' Inge asked. The tree decorations were all I had of sharing Christmas in Norway with Henry.

Softened by what Inge had told me, I thought anything was better than sitting there waiting for news from Henry or V. I was too tired to struggle or maintain my feelings. 'I didn't finish what I was making.'

Inge asked me what I needed and let me choose and cut a length of thick blue wool. She said Lars and I would be allowed out to the workshop with strict instructions to stay put, door closed. I was warmed by her trust and promised I wouldn't go anywhere.

I had taken just about no notice of what Lars had been making and now he hid whatever it was from me, his back hunched as he sat on a stool with his piece of wood on his lap, drilling. I guessed he was avoiding me, afraid to speak to me after what he might have done. I threaded and tied loops of wool in the little Christmas tree ornaments I had made, and decorated them with felt pens that Inge had let me borrow. My temper and frustration had calmed, but my fears had not.

Still with his back to me, Lars spoke first. 'I spoke to Valda from the junk shop earlier. She telephoned the house while you were gone. She said I was only allowed to give the message to you when you were on your own.'

I was immediately glad to hear of V. 'What did she say?'

'She found the hotel where Miss Anders had been staying but she'd gone, although they knew where. Valda went in a taxi to the next hotel because their phone lines were out too, but Miss Anders had already taken a train to Oslo and won't be back until tomorrow.' He delivered all the information clearly. 'Valda left a message for her saying we've found the bear and for Miss Anders to come to her shop as soon as she returns.'

The thought of what V had done to help the bear

made a warm soft spot in my heart. We still had to wait until tomorrow for Miss Anders to come – if the hunters didn't find Bear first – but it was a huge relief to hear help was on its way. And then a small suspicion niggled at me.

'If the phone lines were down, how did V phone here?'

'She's at the hospital.'

'Why?' The thought of V being hurt or ill made me shrink inside. 'What's happened?'

Lars turned round now. 'When she came out of the hotel to get back in the taxi, she slipped on ice and hurt her ankle. She's at the hospital just outside of town now, waiting for an X-ray. Their phone lines are working.'

We needed her but now she was out of action.

'V won't be able to meet Miss Anders at the shop if she's at the hospital,' I said.

'She said she'd work something out and let us know.'

But I cared very much that V was hurt and wanted so much to see for myself that she was okay. Lars must have seen how worried I looked.

'We could go and see her at the hospital and ask what she wants us to do,' Lars offered.

His thoughtfulness surprised and reassured me. 'Maybe she'll ask me to meet Miss Anders instead.' I bit my lip. 'But then I'd have to find a way to escape from the house.'

Lars smiled. 'Don't worry. We'll think of something.'

For a moment all I could think was that every single time I'd had a suspicion about Lars, I had been proved wrong. Had I missed out on a friend all this time? There was one more thing I needed to clear up.

'When Henry went to get in the van, what did you tell him?'

'Nothing. I wanted to go with him but he wouldn't let me.' I knew what it felt like to be overlooked by Henry.

Lars smiled thinly, but I could see that Henry had upset him. Then he looked up at me from under his fringe with a grin. 'Don't worry about the bear,' he said, springing back to his usual bouncy self. 'Henry was going over to the other side of town because I told him Mr Prag and the others were following bear footprints. It's dark now. They'll give up for tonight soon.' My heart melted at his loyalty to our cause.

Quietly, I finished my ornaments under the pool of light from a bare bulb.

Time ticked slowly by while I held out for Henry's return and news from the hunting party. But I didn't hear him come home.

CHAPTER TWENTY-SEVEN

I t was Christmas Eve.

At home, the first thing I would have done would be to wrap a present for Mum, tie it with a ribbon, write all my love in a message on a tag, and, still in my pyjamas, put it under the tree. Before coming to Norway, I had left the present already wrapped under my bed at home ready for her. When I woke on Christmas Eve at Henry's house, my first thought was of Mum looking under my bed. I imagined her putting the gift under the tree, trying to hide her excitement every time she passed it. The thought warmed my heart and made it ache at the same time.

Someone was moving around downstairs.

I tiptoed to the hall and peered through the banisters. At home, this day was for present wrapping, singing songs and carols, a walk into town to see the lights, the aroma of fresh pine from the tree, the glow of the lights reflecting off every surface, turning the darkest of corners gold. We would lay out the old cracked plate with the cheese, biscuits and mince pie for Father Christmas, the carrots for the reindeer, our mugs for hot chocolate. After hanging our stockings, Mum and I would curl up on the sofa and she would read me a story until almost midnight. It was ours, and I felt cherished in the familiarity of it all. At Henry and Inge's house, the only light came from the fire as Henry lit it. But what Inge had told me about their traditions left me with the feeling that although I might not have seen what I expected, the feeling of Christmas was still here.

I thought of Bear. I had no idea what might have happened to him overnight. Thoughts of home paled as I padded downstairs and asked Henry if they'd found the bear.

They hadn't. 'But we did find some strange bear tracks. A bear with two right front feet.'

His brow knitted. My stomach tightened. If they'd not been convinced by the prints, they'd renew their search elsewhere. Might it also send the hunters to another part of the forest? Would they have some idea that they should look on the opposite side of town? Henry squinted but I was giving away nothing, and I wasn't going to betray Lars to him either. Perhaps we had done enough to delay them until Miss Anders arrived.

'The bear isn't dangerous and I have proof,' I said, suddenly desperate for him to believe my *silly* story.

'What do you know about bears?' he said. 'There aren't any in Britain.'

I pulled up my sleeves, kicked out my legs to prove that I had no limbs missing, that I had not been harmed. 'I have been close enough to know that the fur on his shoulders is white at the tip. *I'm* the proof! He didn't hurt me.'

Henry got up from kneeling by the fire. 'If you really did see it, you have to tell me where.' He seemed resigned that I would say no anyway.

I had to give up trying to persuade Henry. It seemed hopeless. But I was not giving up on the bear and what we needed to do to keep him safe. We needed to talk to V and find out what to do next.

Lars was on the stairs. I waved for him to come down, ignoring Henry's question.

'We want to go and see V. She's at the hospital and she should be meeting Miss Anders today who is coming to rescue the bear.' I hoped Henry would clearly understand who I had chosen to be close to now and whose side I was on. 'Inge said you're not working today, so please would you take us to the hospital?'

Henry sighed. But he had no excuse. 'You've got two minutes to get dressed,' he said, and within three minutes we were in his van and shivering in the deep cold of the morning. I had no hat now as I'd left it with Bear. Noticing, Henry offered me his.

It was a small cottage hospital, and although we were too early for visiting hours, the nurses were kind as it was Christmas Eve. We were directed along pale blue corridors to where Valda was in a room with other empty beds, the curtains drawn around her.

'Hello, V? It's Thea.'

'Oh, my darling, thank goodness you're here.' When I pulled the curtain away it was as if a clapperboard had snapped and a director called action. V had turned into her starlet self, propped up on crisp white sheets and pillows. Her hair was rolled in fuzzy curlers, her eyelashes blackened, her lips only outlined and not yet painted, as she was still in the middle of preparing for the day. She wore a long silky kimono gown with boughs of blossom printed on it. I was in awe at each different outward version of herself, and yet she was consistently, uniquely the same V. I must have stared again.

'It's early. I can't be gorgeous the whole time,' she said by way of explanation. Her foot and ankle were plastered and she nodded her head towards it. 'Fractured, I'm afraid.'

'You need some sensible boots,' I said.

She rolled her eyes then smiled. 'Sensible has no passion in it, my darling.' She glanced Henry's way, curtly acknowledging him. 'We don't seem to meet in the same circles.'

Henry twitched uncomfortably. 'Morning,' he offered.

V greeted Lars. 'Inge Pederson must be your mother. I see the resemblance now.'

Lars nodded. 'She comes in your junk shop sometimes.'

V raised her sculpted eyebrows. I shook my head so she'd ignore his description and drew breath, the urgency of the bear's situation rising to the top of my chest again.

'What are we going to do when Miss Anders arrives at your shop?'

'After this frightful business with my ankle, I sent a taxi driver back to the hotel with a note for Miss Anders. I've given her my phone number at the hospital—'

'Did you see the bear?' Henry interrupted.

'Me?' V said, fluttering her eyelashes as she glanced at me. I must have screwed up my face in despair. 'Do I look like I plod around in the woods and the wilds?'

Henry blushed. V narrowed her eyes. She reached to pull me on the side of the bed, and whispered, although not too quietly, 'What else is going on here, darling? I sense a little tension.'

Henry looked up at the ceiling, decidedly uncomfortable at overhearing V's frankness.

'He thinks I made my story up,' I said very quietly.

'Do you know what people say about writers?' V turned to Henry now and he leaned away a little in defence. 'They say that they either write things worth reading or they do things worth writing.' She held his eyes with a strong stare until he glanced away. 'And sometimes, a rare one does both.'

She looked back at me. 'Miss Anders also sent a message back to me with a taxi driver. It'll take a little time today to organize the transport to take the bear to a sanctuary just outside of Oslo. He'll need to be assessed by a vet as they know he is quite old.' She held my hand. 'It's for the best, darling.' How soon the bear might be taken away thumped me in the chest, but at least he'd have somewhere safe to go.

In the meantime, Miss Anders would be taking a train to the town and would meet up with the transport later. As soon as she could make phone contact with V at the hospital again, V would direct her to meet me so I could take her to the bear.

'All that matters is that they're coming.' She looked down for a moment, blinking rapidly, and then up at Henry. 'And the bear will be safe from the likes of Mr Prag.'

I flung my arms around her neck. 'Thank you.'

'Mind my hair, darling,' she whispered, and I patted the curler I had disturbed back into place. 'I should tell you also that I'm sorry but the typewriter wasn't meant for you after all. I sold it to some out-of-towner the day before yesterday. Full price too.'

I looked down at my boots. They were what had caused me such frustration and upset. But because of the boots, I had found the bear and a way to write about something I cared for deeply, and, for a short while, got to use the wonderful typewriter in V's shop.

'It's okay,' I said, and I meant it. 'I can use Mum's. It's not a classic like the Hermes 3000, but it will do.' Henry shifted his feet uncomfortably.

'Now go back to the house and wait there. When Miss Anders gets here, it's all down to you,' V said.

In the meantime, all we could do was wait for Miss Anders. I was not going to find this easy at all.

CHAPTER TWENTY-EIGHT

enry took Lars and me back to the house. He was stonily quiet, and even ignoring the pressing issue of finishing the sledge which he was supposed to deliver today. What else might be going on?

'Where are they looking for the bear today?' I asked Henry as we headed from the van into the house.

'It's Christmas Eve. Most didn't want to be out searching.'

'Most of them?'

'Prag and a couple of others will have gone.' He stopped and faced me properly now. 'He's not good at tracking, if that's what you're worried about. But he is persistent.'

I was torn. If I sneaked out of the house to go to the bear, I might miss Miss Anders' arrival. Any delay in making sure she got to the bear before the hunters was not worth the risk to Bear's life. My fear for him would not go away but it was difficult to weigh up what was best.

'You could tell Mr Prag that Miss Anders is coming,' Lars said to Henry, just as I was thinking the same thing.

'I don't know exactly where he is,' Henry said plainly. 'Probably still following a bear with two right front feet.' We had to take Henry at his word and rely on Mr Prag's incompetence.

The family gathered together. Even with everything going on and being under house arrest,

Elissa was expecting Christmas Eve to follow their normal family tradition. It was the first time I wondered whether Henry had found it easy to fit in with the rest of Inge's family; to fit in anywhere at all. Perhaps I had not only inherited his unruly hair but also some of the unwavering resolve he had over his own passions.

'What about our tree?' Elissa said huffily. 'We *always* go and get our tree from the woods on Christmas Eve. I haven't picked anything to make the table decoration yet either.'

'We can't go out with the bear around, and anyway, I have food to prepare for this evening,' Inge said. 'Henry, what do you suggest?'

'Things are a little different this year.' Henry sat down by the fire and leaned his chin on his hand, his elbow resting on his knee. I could almost hear his brain whirring.

'Have they searched for the bear near here?' Elissa said. 'Maybe it's gone.'

Henry squinted. I could tell these questions were ticking over in his mind but couldn't be sure what conclusion he was coming to.

With nobody sure what to do, Inge asked me and Lars to help her in the kitchen again as Elissa had no interest in cooking at all. We brushed the salt from the herring I'd helped with the day before, rolling and packing it into glass jars with onion, carrot, bay leaves, spices and vinegar. I found I liked being with Inge and I think she appreciated me and Lars joining her when Elissa didn't. My nose was getting used to the different smells of their food, which even made my mouth water. After a while Henry got up and went upstairs. He was gone for some time before some inner instinct stirred in me that all might not be well. I had to know what was going on with him and went upstairs to find him.

I froze in the doorway of my room. Henry was sitting on my bed, my satchel beside him unbuckled, reading the typed sheets of my story. He half-glanced at me, then carried on reading. My first thought was that what I had written would tell him all about me and the bear, and where the cave was.

'It's a story. It doesn't mean it's true,' I said. I realized in horror that I had described precisely where the bear was hidden. 'It's a silly story!' I used his words now to protect the bear in case he chose to find Mr Prag and tell him.

'But it is true, isn't it?' His voice crackled.

I felt desperate that he might use my writing to hurt the bear. 'Even if it is, you don't believe he's a good bear.'

'I mean, the whole thing is true. The bits about me . . .'

This was not a part of the story I had intended Henry to *ever* read. My heart galloped, remembering the horrible, angry things I'd written.

Henry turned the last sheet over, picked them

all up and looked at the first page again. My stomach sank.

'Stories are a kind of mixture of make-believe—' I began. No matter how far apart Henry and I had drifted, it would be awful for anyone to read about themselves like that. Was he angry? Now that he believed it was the truth, could I convince him to save Bear?

Henry's eyes lowered to the floor.

'The bear smells like an old rug. He drools when he eats and spills food all over himself. His breath is really bad. And he looks scary, but only if you're scared of him,' I said in a rush, trying to gather back something more than the bad feelings. 'But I love him.' Henry looked up. My lip trembled, my eyes filled. 'And I don't want anyone to hurt the bear, and now you've read about him I'm worried that's what you are going to do. I wanted a good story. I wanted a good ending.'

Henry put the sheets down and stood up.

He wouldn't look at me. He murmured, 'It's good writing.'

'It's not finished.'

He held my eyes for all of five seconds, then left the room, hurrying down the stairs. And as I stood there, frozen to the spot, horror creeping into every ounce of me, the front door closed behind him.

I ran downstairs after him and over to the window. I had gone too far. My words, my writing . . . what had I done to us and the bear?

'Thea, you must stay here,' Inge said, catching me before I went after Henry.

Henry got in the van and drove off, the van skidding a little on the ice on the driveway.

'What's wrong with Henry?' Elissa said.

As I continued to stare out of the window at the van disappearing around the corner, I could not believe what else I saw.

Bear was coming down the road towards the house.

CHAPTER TWENTY-NINE

Bear was magnificently huge out in the road without the giant stature of great trees in the woods to compare him to. But the sight of him by the house froze my heart. Henry might return any minute. What if he arrived with Mr Prag? Bear sniffed the air and the ground as he plodded towards the house. Elissa screamed from beside me and everyone rushed to the window while I slipped outside, hardly able to breathe for what might happen next.

As I hurried down the sloping drive, I slipped on the ice and landed on my knees and hands. I couldn't get a grip and slid all the way down until I knocked into Bear's feet.

Inge immediately opened the door and came out, still holding the door handle, her back flat against the door, whispering, 'Oh, Thea! Stay very still!'

Bear glanced up at the faces in the window and at Inge who had now grabbed a broom. I only knew him in the small magical world we had created, and although I could not help but fill with joy at seeing him, fear of what he might do crept into me. I had no idea whether the gentle side of him was only for me, whether he might see anybody else as a threat and lash out. Bear groaned and stamped his feet.

'Don't do anything sudden or loud, Thea,' Inge whispered urgently. 'Can you get up? Move slowly. I'm coming.'

My heart was pounding although I wasn't afraid

of Bear, only what he might be capable of doing if he felt threatened. 'I'm okay,' I said, rolling over.

I had to persuade Bear to come away but I had no food to coax him and my knee hurt and I couldn't get a grip on the ice. I fell back down when I tried to stand.

'It's okay, Bear, you're with me,' I told him softly to calm him. I was about to ask Inge to get some food, throw it away from the house, but she was already stepping slowly towards me, holding the end of the broom out for me to grab hold. Bear swayed his head, groaned and huffed great billows of air, as if preparing for something bigger. I remembered the stick I'd waved when I first met him in the woods, how scared Bear had been. Would he be scared of the broom handle? Was he preparing to attack the one holding it now he was in unfamiliar territory?

'Put the broom down!' I whispered to Inge. 'He doesn't want to hurt me but he might think you will hurt him.'

She shook her head, her eyes wide, and I pleaded again. At last she laid it down. 'Okay, Thea,' she said, her voice soft and comforting. She wanted me to know that she would help me in any way she could. I turned back to Bear.

'You're a good bear,' I said. 'Nobody is going to hurt you.'

With the threat seemingly gone, Bear calmed and looked down at me. Then Inge could hardly believe her eyes when he lay down beside me. The magic of him allowing us to be so close thrilled me all over again, especially as Inge was here to see and believe what I had tried to tell everyone about the amazing bear.

Inge's hand closed over her mouth, her eyes in a panic, but she could only stare as I held on to Bear's fur and he pulled me back upright with him. He lowered his head and sniffed at my knee where the jeans had ripped and my skin had grazed, stinging as pearls of blood formed.

Inge's chest was heaving as she blinked back tears.

'The bear helped you. I saw it with my own eyes,' she whispered in astonishment.

Lars opened the door. 'I want to see him,' he said, while Elissa held firmly to his sleeve, her mouth gaping open too.

'Why did you come here, Bear?' I said, his anxiety seemingly gone, now that he was in my company. 'Did you smell the herrings?'

'Thea,' Inge said, taking another step closer. 'Come inside, let me look at your knee.'

The pain had all but disappeared as there were other more pressing matters suddenly crushing my chest. I looked up and down the road. I needed to get Bear out of sight. I closed my eyes for a long, long blink, trying to make the urgency of Bear's situation vanish. I couldn't do it all on my own.

I looked at Inge, Lars and Elissa. 'This is the worst place for the bear to be right now,' I said. 'I think Henry might have gone to get Mr Prag because he knows where Bear's cave is. He'll come back this way. Please will you all help me make Bear safe?'

That same dark look passed over Lars's face that I had seen when Henry left the house, but he spoke before I could ask him what was the matter.

'We can hide him out the back for a while and maybe think of an idea, together,' Lars said. We made a trail of biscuits, taking Bear through the gate at the side of the house that led to the back garden. I limped a short distance behind Bear, closing the gate to keep us out of sight.

Bear sat down where Inge had left herrings for him on the snow. I joined the others gathered together talking quietly by the back door.

'I told Inge and Elissa what you said at the meeting. And about Miss Anders,' Lars said. 'I've got some more herring for the bear.' He had armfuls of jars.

'Tip it on the ground and then step back,' I told Lars. 'He won't hurt you.' I swiped a pillow of snow from the stone garden bench and sat down to watch, to think.

Lars tipped out the herring then sat on the bench beside me. Elissa and Inge joined us, but I barely registered what was going on. I needed to watch the bear for a minute, to let the wonder of him fill me up, emptying out all the distress that blocked my clear thinking before I could move on.

Bear ate hungrily, licking scales and vinegar from between his toes when he suddenly seemed to remember we were there and took his time to look at each one of us. I felt some reassurance that he only looked at us as company, bringing what he needed, not threatening to hurt him.

'He makes me shiver,' Lars whispered.

Elissa laughed. 'Me too.'

It was the first time I had seen Elissa look happy. While we were in the bear's company, we were distracted from ourselves and our discomfort with each other. None of us seemed like strangers and

I didn't feel separated from them any more. Inge popped in and out of the house, bringing a dish of sliced cucumber, cooked cabbage and sour-cream porridge left over from this morning. Bear licked it all up, looking over at us, as if he was part of this circle too, a dribble of porridge on his chin that he searched out with his tongue. And when I looked at Lars and Elissa, the distance between all of us seemed gone.

'Just so you know, the bear has eaten your Christmas supper.' Inge laughed.

'I don't mind. It's like Santa Claus came to visit,' Elissa said. It was nice to see her like this, excited and in wonder. Perhaps she hadn't seen it in me before either. We had not met this best side of each other. I warmed to her now.

'You mean Father Christmas,' Lars said, looking at me to back him up.

'I *mean* Santa Claus,' Elissa said.

'It's the same difference,' I said with a smile, and

Elissa shrugged. There wasn't enough fuel left to create an argument or keep our opposition going now Bear had made us forget our grievances. He was greater than all of us.

Elissa and Lars were different. Without scowls and suspicions and jealousy about Henry, it all seemed so much easier. I wondered, had we all been envious of each other? They had Henry in their lives now, and I knew it couldn't be easy for them either. And perhaps I shouldn't have asked anything of him that he wasn't willing to give. Not even a typewriter.

Bear had come a little closer but none of us moved. Standing on all fours, he stared at each of us with that powerful intensity that made us forget he was a bear and we were children. It felt as if we were the same as him in many ways, and we were so much more to each other in that togetherness.

CHAPTER THIRTY

'What's "good bear" in Norwegian?' I asked.

'*God bjørn*,' Elissa said. 'And he is, isn't he?' She smiled as if our ill will towards each other had never existed.

Inge came out of the house again. 'Does he like waffles?'

'Who doesn't?' Lars said.

Inge left them for us to give to Bear and went back inside, at ease leaving us with our huge friend while she pulled together more food from the cupboards. Perhaps I should have asked Inge to make the gingerbread house. How wrong I had been about everyone.

Elissa, Lars and I smiled, at the bear scoffing the waffles, at each other. I realized that Christmas didn't need snow or trees or tinsel. It was about coming together like this. Here was the magic.

Inge suddenly opened the kitchen window. 'Mr Prag and some others are coming from the woods!'

I tensed as it struck me that I was more terrified knowing how close they were to discovering Bear's whereabouts than I had been facing the bear that first time. The hunters must have found Bear's prints and followed them here.

Bear sniffed deeply at the air, snorted and groaned deeply in his throat. His great paws stamped the ground as if unsure.

'What can we do?' I breathed, my heart thumping wildly.

'We could tell them he's tame,' Elissa said.

'Thea already tried that,' Lars said, looking at me. 'I have an idea. Feed the bear something he really likes to keep him occupied.' He slipped away from us, out of the gate, closing it behind him, and Elissa ran back to the house for more food.

I could hear Lars and Mr Prag talking in Norwegian on the driveway. Bear took in huge snorts of air, no doubt picking up the scent of all the people outside. He came closer to the gate, groaning, swaying as if he sensed he might be trapped.

I was panicking now that I couldn't get in front of him because he filled the narrow passageway between the house and the workshop. He was powerful enough to take down the gate. And even if he didn't, they might hear him growling and puffing.

Elissa returned with a tray of all sorts of food and I spoke to Bear, soothing him, coaxing him away from the gate with a trail of food. He followed but his ears twitched back.

'Elissa, can you go by the gate and listen to what they are saying? Is Henry with them?'

'I don't think he is . . .' Elissa turned her head and tucked her hair behind her ear. 'Prag said they followed bear prints out of the woods, just up the road from here . . . Henry isn't out there because Prag is asking where Henry is and why he didn't join the search party.' It wasn't Henry who sent them here? 'Lars is saying that Miss Anders is coming so there's no need to keep searching.'

Bear turned his head away from the food and snorted again, puffing up, seeming bigger. He growled deeply.

'Mr Prag heard that!' Elissa whispered urgently.

'Please, Bear, we're trying to help you. Shh!' How do you tell a bear to be quiet?

'Lars is saying that you are out in the garden playing a game of bears.' Elissa was as surprised as I was at his imagination. I really had got Lars completely wrong. He was so invested in doing anything to stand by the bear, and all of us. If I could have taken back everything mean I had said and done to him I would have.

'Now Prag is saying . . .' Elissa said. 'Oh, never mind, I won't repeat that. Now Lars is telling him you're going to be a writer. Are you?' My heart grew like a baking cake.

'Yes, I am . . . I was.' Although with the damage it had done to Henry and me I wasn't sure if I should ever write again.

'Lars is saying that Henry has gone to deliver the sledge, but . . . when he comes back, he's not joining the hunting parties. He is going to spend time with his family.' Elissa sighed. 'I doubt he will though.'

Henry was consistently Henry, no matter who he lived with, but even the mention of him snagged my stomach. What was he doing?

Lars stayed out at the front for a few minutes before coming back to tell us they had gone towards town. He had said he guessed Henry had gone to deliver the sledge but there was a dark shadow on his face again.

'You did a good job of buying us some time, Lars,' I said. He beamed, but only for a moment.

'I don't think Mr Prag is going to give up.' Lars seemed more anxious than I'd thought he could be. 'I don't trust him to not come back again. I don't think he believed what I said because he seemed suspicious.'

'Lars, what's wrong? Please tell me.'

He stared at me for a moment. 'I saw Henry put his gun in the van.'

I was barely able to speak or breathe. Surely he wouldn't . . . I could think of nothing more unforgiveable than the bear dying at Henry's hands.

'Lars, we've got to get Bear out of here before either Mr Prag or Henry comes back.' Lars nodded.

He must have had that same bleak thought as me.

Inge came running outside. 'Miss Anders just telephoned! Valda gave her the number. She's on her way here by train and the lorry is coming from Oslo.' We so desperately needed to hear this. 'But it's going to take a couple of hours for them all to get here. I'll pick her up from the station but the lorry won't be here until around six this evening.'

It was too long to wait here.

'Lars?' His eyes were glued to the magnificence of the great bear snuffling in the snow for crumbs. 'Where's Henry's cabin?'

'It's not too far.'

'Would you let me take the bear to Henry's cabin, Inge?' I asked. I found I *did* want her approval, her support. 'I'll hide there with Bear for now until Miss Anders gets here. He won't be safe here.' My voice grew shaky. 'And Henry knows where Bear's cave is now so I can't take him there.'

Inge put her arms around me in a strong hug and I sank into it.

'You have a good heart, Thea, and I think you are desperate to use it,' she said. 'You can be sure that we are all with you and on the bear's side too. What do you need?'

CHAPTER THIRTY-ONE

The bear had grown used to relying on humans, responding to them in any way which placated them, but he was not and never would be one of them. Something had changed in him. Some of that wildness was coming back to him. The people here gave him what he needed, and he was growing stronger. He was old and tired, but he could survive now.

Bear would have sensed something of the growing danger around him. But he would not have known our fears were for him, and not ourselves.

Lars told me Henry's cabin was easy to find, once you knew how to get there. Henry didn't know they all knew where it was and it had been a standing family secret between them. Lars volunteered to scout the area for any hunters coming this way while Inge would wait for Miss Anders and collect her from the station which was about twenty miles away, bring her back to the house to meet the lorry and other members of the organization responsible for rescuing animals. Elissa would stay at the house in case anyone phoned with important messages or if Henry came back, in which case she would misdirect him too until more help arrived.

We all agreed that I'd need a good supply of food for the bear, to get him to follow me, to keep him happy. We left him with more waffles in the garden and went into the house. Inge made me warm by the fire while she bathed and dressed the graze on my knee. Lars had found his skiing trousers for me to wear, which were padded like the coat, and I still had Henry's hat. I put on double socks, an extra jumper and wore my satchel out of habit, and went to the workshop for snowshoes Inge said I might need. I put the tree ornaments in my satchel, thinking I could hang them in Henry's cabin, make a little bit of Christmas for Bear and me in our last few hours together. Maybe I'd sing Christmas carols for him again.

The sledge was still in the workshop. The fact that it was still there confirmed that Henry was not on a delivery. I accepted with a heavy heart now that Henry, the hunter, was not the one that I could have asked for help.

Inge and Elissa met me in the workshop. They had collected some food and water for me, blankets, a first aid kit, a sleeping bag, much more food for the bear and other just-in-case items.

'I'm only going to be there a couple of hours,' I said.

'Yes, but we want to make sure you're both warm and fed,' Inge said.

'What I meant was that I can't carry it all.'

Inge was insistent that I needed all these things. And then we all stopped and stared at what was in front of us. The sledge was beautifully made, separate pieces of wood joined together in an almost miraculous, seamless whole.

'Do you think the bear could pull the sledge?' Inge said. 'Lars told me what you'd said about his life with the militants. His behaviour is not what I'd expect from a bear, but if you think he'd be okay to do it, then I'd be happy that you both had the supplies you might need.' She was concerned that if Miss Anders was delayed or it snowed, the bear and I might be stuck out at the cabin for longer than we expected. 'Just in case,' she said.

We all looked at each other for a moment. I wasn't

sure I wanted to remind Bear of his past.

'We could try, and if the bear doesn't look happy then we'll just forget it,' Elissa said. 'But what will Henry say when he finds the sledge missing?' I was thinking the same thing.

Inge lay her palm flat against her forehead but didn't think too long. 'I'll deal with Henry. Let's give it a try.'

We towed the sledge to the back garden. Bear stopped licking between his toes and looked at us with great interest. Inge picked up a harness, unbuckling some straps and fastening others.

Bear stood up, as if he knew what was about to be asked of him, and watched while Inge quickly combined harness straps meant for much smaller-chested huskies to make one long enough to wrap over his shoulders and around his chest. Thrilled and not yet able to shake off all her fears, Elissa tentatively passed the strap under him and I buckled it on the other side.

'I know you've done this before, Bear,' I told him quietly. 'We aren't going to do anything to hurt anyone.'

Lars went off down the road to see if the coast was clear while Elissa packed the sledge and covered it with a plastic sheet. I climbed up on the sledge seat, held the reins, just as Lars came running back, panting.

'I saw Mr Prag!' My breath caught at the top of my chest. Inge reached for my hand and we held on tight.

'Where exactly is he?' she asked Lars.

'He's on his own now and has stopped at someone's house down the road but it looks like he's heading this way again. You have to get going, Thea!'

Lars ran down the drive again, looked each way several times, then waved his arm for us to come out of the drive. Inge opened the gate.

'Keep our girl safe, dear bear,' she said.

Elissa had her arms wrapped around herself. 'See

you soon, Thea,' she said.

A little time spent with the bear and my head was now clear. I knew what I had to do.

Lars beckoned Bear with the last jar of herrings. Bear hesitated a little as he sensed the weight he had to pull behind him, but I encouraged him to go forward and as soon as the sledge touched the ice on the drive it slipped smoothly along.

'You're a good spy, Lars. Thank you,' I called, but he was already running back down the road.

Bear was soon accustomed to the sledge, quickening his step and lumbering along the track. I steered by pulling the reins on either side and tucked my chin into the collar of the coat against the cold air as Bear got into his stride and the sledge found its smooth feet on the snow.

We turned into the woods and the wilds, to go further than the forest edge to where the snow lay untouched and we wouldn't be found by anyone we didn't want.

Lacy snowflakes fell as Bear and I took the route Lars had shown me on a map. Above us, the bank of cloud descended to veil the tips of the tallest trees. The further we went, the deeper the snow was, but the sledge was at home on this surface and Bear was strong. He crushed the snow with his wide hairy legs and paws, and on we went as the snow continued to gently fall and hopefully begin to cover our tracks. I

had not imagined that I would be so lucky as to have some more time with him, to say a proper goodbye, to be happy for a while longer. I would not let my imagination run away into thoughts of how Miss Anders would have to take him away, how he would feel to be captured again.

I blinked snowflakes from my eyelashes as my breath turned into droplets of water that then froze on my hair as it escaped out of Henry's hat. The day wasn't yet drawing in but the light had faded even further

in the shadows of the trees. The sky was thickening with dove-grey clouds, blindfolding the sun, and the temperature was dropping. My heart stayed warm because I would always have this memory of Christmas Eve in a winter wonderland with a bear.

Lars had told me to keep going straight on until we came out of the woods and the wilds, to keep a mountain with a sharp peak to my right, to find an open plain where the forest was to my left. Then I had to look out for a ring of stumps and turn right. There would be a wide-open track through a dense pine forest. The cabin was fairly hidden in the forest but a pair of stumps had been placed at the edge of the track to indicate where to go into the trees.

'Keep going straight on then, and you'll come to it,' he'd told me. His instructions were clear and within half an hour we had found the cabin.

CHAPTER THIRTY-TWO

enry's cabin was as big as a garage, fringed with icicles, clad with halves of timber and pale bark. The door wasn't locked. I didn't suppose anybody went out this way very often. There was a log store to the side, half-filled, an axe and stump for splitting logs, but no footprints to say that Henry had been here recently. I peered through the window before going in.

There was little more than a woodburning stove, a single bed, a workbench, sawdust and tools, and a wooden chair. The arms of the chair were smooth as skin, the seat generous and the back curved. There was no doubt that Henry had made it.

A kettle and one tin cup were on the stove. There was no electricity, no running water, but plenty of matches and candles. It was familiar to me as Henry's spaces had always been, but he was not. I wondered if he would be upset with me for saving the bear, for using his cabin to protect it. Deep inside there was a sadness that our differences had now put us in opposition and the distance between us had become so great that I doubted we could ever reconnect.

Bear stood in the doorway sniffing the air inside the cabin. He would have to come in too and stay out of sight. I coaxed him through the doorway with blueberries and biscuits.

I lit candles until it felt homely and set about making a fire. I wished I'd had a demonstration from Lars but was smart enough to use some kindling from a basket and some smaller logs to get it going. I copied what I'd seen Henry doing and banked up the fire until the heat pulsed into the room. I scraped snow from outside into the kettle and found teabags, milk powder and sugar in jars, and while the water boiled and Bear ate, I decorated the cabin with the tree ornaments. They weren't the kind of decorations I had been used to with Mum, but these were just for us and that made them special.

As the cabin warmed, icicles dripped from outside and Bear's journey here had tired him out. He lay on a mat in front of the stove while I sat on the wooden chair with the tea.

'It won't be long now,' I told Bear. 'Soon, you'll be safe.' I thought about Miss Anders, making her way here through the snow, and hoped I was right.

In the quiet and warmth and glow of the fire I think I understood why Henry came here. Without the danger to Bear, it would have made a perfect writer's cabin too. With no disturbances, and the beautiful whiteness of the surrounding forest, I could be myself, free to imagine, free to express my deepest thoughts. I wondered if after this holiday I would ever see Henry again, if he would ever want to see me. I remembered what my mother had said, that I should pursue my dreams of both becoming a writer and finding a way to get closer to Henry, but that I might have to accept he would, in the end, not have a hand in either of these things. What she told me finally settled, as if the words had been falling all this time and had now landed in a place where I could understand. And that meant I'd had to live them first. I could be a writer without Henry's support, encouragement or pride, or the typewriter. It was down to me to understand that, to keep my heart open to its possibility, no matter what came my way. When I got home, I'd write the rest of this story, the ending Bear deserved.

Low clouds descended further and swathed the cabin in mist while the snow fell silently but thickly. Bear was sleeping soundly, his lips fluttering slightly when he breathed out with a soft growl of a snore. There was no clock and I had no watch, but time disappeared as I lay down on the mat with him and watched him sleep and loved him for a couple more hours.

Bear's eyes blinked open. He sniffed the air. The fur on his shoulders bristled and a growl rumbled in his throat. I knew Bear's nose and ears would sense someone approaching long before I did. He rose to his feet, shaking out his fur, taking deep breaths, his shoulders high and taut like I'd not seen before. My heart began to race, not only at the wildness that seemed to be returning to the bear, but because I could not tell whether it was his rescuers or the hunters that were coming.

I put on my coat and opened the door a little and looked out. I shone the torch but looking through the falling snow and shadows and cloud was like trying to see through a net curtain. In the distance, I heard a swooshing sound, an engine like a motorbike, the flash of a light.

'Stay there,' I told Bear, holding my hand up to him. I closed the door to keep him hidden while I stepped outside. I was prepared to defend the bear in any way I could if I had to.

The sound and light were coming closer, rushing towards the cabin. It didn't sound quite right for a lorry but whatever it was flickered through the trees, moving quickly. Eventually it was close enough that I could make out it was a snowmobile, Henry riding it.

Henry came to a halt and turned the engine off.

'Lars told me where you were,' he called. After

everything that had happened, I didn't believe Lars would have betrayed us, but why would he have led Henry to me and the bear?

'Stay away!' I shouted to Henry. My scalp prickled and my heart raced at what I might have to do to keep Henry out. 'I don't want you here!'

'I haven't brought Prag with me. He doesn't know where I am. I've brought Miss Anders,' Henry said, stepping off the snowmobile.

I had not seen Miss Anders at first, hidden as she was behind Henry, and he held his hand out to help her off the back of the seat.

'Miss Anders!' I said to the woman in the yellow coat.

'Call me Jennifer,' she said. 'I know who you are, Thea. Your family told me. We couldn't get the lorry through the track and it's being driven around a different route. Henry said it was urgent that we get to you sooner. I believe you found the bear,' she said. 'I'm so relieved.' She blinked through the snow with bright twinkling eyes, as I looked to Henry.

'But . . .' It was Henry that I had not expected. 'I thought . . .'

'Don't forget I read your story,' he said. 'And you need a good ending to write about.'

CHAPTER THIRTY-THREE

More than anything, I was astounded at Henry's change of heart, and the fact that it was because of my story. Hurtful as it was to him, he had put that to one side, for my sake and the bear's. As Henry, Miss Anders and I stood there in the snow and the clouds, in the silence of the winter forest, the night swooped in like a giant dark-winged bird, its shadow falling upon the whole forest.

From behind me, Bear banged against the door.

He growled and groaned because there was a scent that was terrifyingly familiar to him. It smelled metallic, and like burned trees.

I thought perhaps it was Henry that Bear might not be at ease with, or the sound of the snowmobile.

'I think it's because he doesn't know you,' I said, my voice wavering. I had not heard his wildness like this before. 'It's okay, Bear. You're going to be safe,' I called to him, hoping my voice would calm him.

Miss Anders said that the lorry might still take a couple more hours to get here. She was not yet sure whether they'd be able to bring the vehicle all the way across the snow, but help was definitely on its way.

'I think he'll come with me,' I said, growing less sure as Bear's growls grew deeper and his claws scraped repeatedly against the door. 'I might be able to lead him to them if they can't get here.'

Henry seemed anxious. 'He doesn't sound very friendly right now.'

Bear suddenly stopped. I was running back to the cabin, when I heard what Bear must have heard all along. There was a sharp *click*, somewhere to my left in the trees. When the land is covered with snow, sound travels in a different way. It's sharp; it brings sounds to you clearly. I heard it, but did not know what it was or how to react to it. But with visibility so poor, I wonder how I must have looked from a distance. Wearing my big brown puffy coat with the hood now up over Henry's hat, I could have appeared to be a small bear.

But Bear had heard that sound before.

The door to the cabin split and crashed open. Bear came hurtling at me, bellowing, his jaws wide, his teeth bared as he roared.

Out of the corner of my eye, I saw Miss Anders reach out to hold Henry's arm. He shook her loose and ran towards me too, his arms above his head, shouting with full force, *'Nei, bjørn!'* ('No, bear!').

Charging at full pelt, Bear reached me before

Henry. With a sweep of his great paw he knocked me off my feet and sent me flying through the air. I landed with a soft *thump* and sank into the snow.

Bear stood up on his hind legs, towering over me, and roared, his body shaking with ferocity.

As Bear drew breath to bellow again, a violent *crack* split the air. His breath came out in a *whump* as it was knocked out of him. He swayed, stumbled, but drew himself up to full height again, still standing on his legs, and bellowed with all his might again.

Having reached me, Henry skidded in the snow, looking up first at the bear and then down at me, and threw himself across me.

I knew what had happened now. I knew what I'd heard.

'He saved me,' I cried to Henry.

And Henry, seeing where the real danger was coming from, got up and ran on, shouting, as Bear continued to stand like a fort in front of me. Another slow *click* burned through the still air once again. Henry didn't stop. He kept running towards a fleck of red and darkness among the woods and the wilds and tackled the man holding the rifle. He snatched the rifle from him as the gun fired into the trees, snow erupting from the branches. Henry punched him in the nose. Mr Prag got up and ran.

Mr Prag had followed in his father's footsteps and shot this bear when he had no need to.

Beside me, raspberry coloured drips were seeping into the snow. With the threat gone, Bear came down heavily on all fours. Blood ran down his left shoulder. He sagged to one side and his breathing came quickly. He moaned, his eyes closed, and he collapsed into the snow.

I pulled myself up and crawled to him and opened my arms.

'No, don't die, please don't die!' After everything we had gone through, I could not lose him now. I put my arms around his great golden head and giant powerful nose and beautiful, beautiful warm brown fur.

'*God, god bjørn*,' I whispered. 'Please don't go.'

I pressed my ear to his side to listen for his heart. It was still beating, but so slowly, his breath shallow.

Henry had run back over. He saw the stain in the snow. 'Are you hurt?' he asked, as tears streamed down my cheeks.

I took off my hat – Henry's hat – and pressed it against Bear's wound. Henry knelt down and held me while I held Bear. I stopped counting how long we stayed like that.

CHAPTER THIRTY-FOUR

The end of the story that I hoped for was that Miss Anders would come and save the bear, but that's not how things turned out. We waited for a while for help to come, to take Bear to safety, but the lorry that was supposed to transport him didn't arrive. We had staunched the flow of Bear's blood with Henry's hat and Miss Anders felt sure that the bullet had not hit any major organs. But Bear's shoulder was ragged from the wound where the bullet had gone right through, and there was no way he could have walked anywhere to meet the transport if they couldn't get here.

Miss Anders decided she would take the snowmobile and find another solution. Miss Anders had made enough difficult rescues to turn her hand to whatever the situation needed. She was seventy-three years old, Henry later told me, and her fearlessness had grown with practice.

Henry stayed with me and the bear, while Miss Anders set off to go to his house to use the phone and make whatever arrangements she could.

Eventually Bear's eyes opened. He panted. He groaned. The frown had returned, creasing between his eyes, and I stroked his head to comfort him. He was tired and weak and yet I had seen the power and fearlessness in him that had been squashed for so long. It had showed itself when it was most needed.

'We need to get him inside,' Henry said. He left us for a short while, to relight the fire in the cabin, to nail some boards across to hold the broken door together.

The snow had turned our coats white as it settled upon me and Bear. No matter how much he might hurt, I had to get him out of the snow.

'You have to get up now, Bear.' I stood up, showing him what I wanted him to do. He blinked. His breathing was still laboured. He would die in the cold without help. I held back all my tears so he would listen to me.

'Get up, Bear!'

He rocked himself more upright before pushing up to a sitting position, holding his paw up under his damaged shoulder. He moaned and growled.

'I know you can do it. It's not far and we'll be warm. That's my dad, Henry. He'll keep us safe.' I walked ahead, turning back, but kept going even when Bear looked like he'd give up, steeling myself against my fears to persuade him that I was not giving up either.

His head hung but he rocked again, pulling himself up on to three legs, and limped carefully, one step at a time, to join Henry and me in the cabin, leaving a dark red trail behind him. He lay down slowly at first then fell on his side in front of the stove. I was so afraid I would lose him, that I had not been able to make him safe.

We checked his wound, cleaned it with warm water, kept pressure against it with Henry's hat, with my scarf and gloves, to stop the bleeding, staying focused and quietly doing everything we could to keep him alive. The snow on us turned to water, to steam, and misted the windows.

Bear wouldn't eat or drink the water I offered him, but blinked against the pain. His breathing relaxed and he lay still as we checked again and again until the bleeding stopped.

'I think he's going to be all right,' Henry said at last. 'Although it'll take a bit of time yet.' He was sitting in his chair. It fitted the contours of his body perfectly.

'I didn't know where you'd gone when you left the house,' I said, inviting Henry to fill in the gaps. Although Miss Anders had told me how they came to be here, I wanted to hear it from Henry himself.

'I needed some time to think,' he said, clasping his hands together before looking me straight in the eyes with an openness that I'd never seen before. 'I admire the kind of brave honesty which you wrote in your story. I see the same kind of honesty in the trees, in the wood I work with . . . then at least I know where I am.' Everything that I needed to know about how we were connected was there in that moment, even without any more words. I accepted it as the best a man who found words hard could do.

He smiled. 'Are you going to write about this too?'

'Yes, I am,' I said.

'Good. Good. Well, I suppose I'd quite like to read the ending sometime.' He hadn't said sorry to me for the hurt he must have known I felt. But we seemed to have reached some understanding now, thanks to Bear bringing us together.

Our attention went to Bear who grumbled

through the pain and needed the crease smoothed out of his head.

'It's Christmas Eve,' Henry said. He bent down to reach under the bed and handed me a slim box he'd made. 'It's for pencils or pens, or whatever you want it for. I don't want anything back, mind.'

Henry had made me a pencil box, soft and polished to a warm bear-brown, with the shape of a tree seamlessly inlaid in the lid in a lighter coloured wood. And when I opened it a rich smell of the forest rose to remind me where it came from.

I would not have swapped it for a typewriter of any kind.

Bear's ears twitched and he raised his head a little, sniffing at the air. We heard chiming in the forest. Christmas bells.

I jumped up and went to the door and looked out, Henry behind me. Three torches bobbed their way towards us.

Henry hummed a gentle groan. Inge, Elissa and

Lars were coming, carrying hiking packs on their backs decorated with bells. Elissa had brought a bunch of woodland evergreens and pine cones, tied with ribbon, and Lars trailed a small Christmas tree that he'd chopped down himself.

I was so happy they had come to join us and welcomed them in.

'Please don't be disappointed that we're all here,' Inge said to Henry. 'It's Christmas Eve and we should be together.'

Lars planted his tree in a bucket of snow outside the door.

'I only made one thing for Christmas,' Lars said. 'I don't think I'm going to be any good at carpentry.' He blushed, his head down, his eyes glancing up at Henry then away. 'But I am a bit proud of myself for trying.'

Lars had made a star. Not the kind of star you might expect, but definitely unique. Hewn from a block of wood, its angles and points were neither uniform nor completely smooth. There were random holes, drilled all the way through, and he'd poked a string of Christmas tree lights into each hole, gathering the loose flex into a knotty bundle at the back.

There was nowhere to plug it in out at the cabin. 'It's too heavy to go on the tree.' Lars sighed as the delicate branches threatened to snap.

Dear Lars had also been trying to find some connection with Henry through wood.

'It's a piece of sculpture, son,' Henry said. And I knew then too that, instead of being jealous, it was more important for me to understand that Henry called Lars 'son' as his way of connecting with him. And I was happy for that.

I think Lars knew what Henry was trying to tell him. He grinned and held the star out, tilting his head to one side, and tried out a few different places before leaning it against the bucket under the tree. It wasn't where you'd expect to find a star, but somehow it seemed perfect for this one Christmas.

CHAPTER THIRTY-FIVE

We huddled in the cabin around Bear in the warm light of the candles and fire, prepared to stay the night together while help was promised for tomorrow. Miss Anders had made it back to the house, and overnight she'd secure arrangements for a different kind of transport to get the bear out of the wilds and a vet to help with his injury. Bear was exhausted and needed to rest and recover but he kept his eyes open to see where he was, and we showed him there was nothing to fear.

'I made this for you, Thea,' Elissa said. 'Happy Christmas.' She'd knitted me a long striped scarf in shades of blue.

I thanked her. 'But it's not Christmas until tomorrow.'

'We do Christmas differently around here,' she said. 'And besides, I think you need it.'

Inge had knitted me socks.

I was unprepared, to say the least. But I gave them each one of the wooden tree ornaments and they seemed genuinely pleased. They asked me about Christmas back home. It was nothing like this year, but this one would be unforgettable. We glowed in the light of the candles and the miracle that we had found with Bear.

Later, we all curled into sleeping bags, close like a tin of sardines, circling our bear. We still wore our clothes, our socks and hats. Nobody complained. They sang Norwegian Christmas songs and Bear was soothed by the sound. *He* made me love them.

There was ice on the windows, floorboards for our beds, no tinsel, no twinkling lights, but Christmas was there because we were as one, brought together by a good bear.

When I woke and it was growing light, both Henry and the bear were gone. I quickly put on coat, boots and hat and went outside. Henry had given the bear blueberries and a whole salmon and was watching as he propped himself gingerly in the snow, his appetite still reassuringly alive.

A new feeling bloomed in my heart, as light as sunshine, when I saw them together that morning.

I went over to Henry and put my arms around his waist and lay my face against his broad chest.

'Happy Christmas,' I said. He put his arms around me. I counted to twenty. To thirty. To forty, and more. He didn't let go until it was enough.

Lars came out of the cabin and took a picture of Henry and the bear with his paw raised as he licked off blueberry juice.

Soon a deep rumble of an engine echoed through the still forest in the distance.

'They're coming,' Henry said. Sadness welled up, knowing that my time with the bear was almost over. 'It's for the best, Thea.'

Bear's ears twitched towards the sound but he looked to Henry and then at me, for a long time. His eyes were clear and bright.

Whether it was his injury, his old age or that he had nothing left to fear, we would never know why he didn't react to his rescuers and was still licking blueberries from the snow when they gave him an injection so he'd sleep and not be scared of his journey. Miss Anders said he was lucky to be alive, that his wasted body had probably only survived because of the food I had given him. They'd do their best for him, they promised. He'd have nothing to fear ever again.

I didn't say goodbye to Bear while he lay down and his eyes blinked slowly as he drifted off to sleep. I sang 'Silent Night' to him. I remembered all the words.

He would never be allowed to roam wild. Humans had taken that life from him, but on Christmas Day of 1978, Miss Anders and her friends took the bear to a sanctuary. They gave him a wide open area with enough trees and bushes and space so he'd have a little of all the freedom that he deserved.

When I returned to Britain, I spent a lot of time finishing the story, typing it up on Mum's typewriter when she brought it home at the weekends.

Lars wrote to me sometimes. He sent me that one and only photo of Henry and Bear. I wrote to Henry using Mum's typewriter when I could, sometimes sending stories. He telephoned me more often, but it was usually me talking, him growling, sometimes asking me a question. We shared what we could with one another. I knew that was as much as I could ask of him.

In the autumn of the following year, Henry sent me a letter.

Bear had died peacefully, lying below a great spruce tree.

CHAPTER THIRTY-SIX

Ursula kneels at the foot of the Christmas tree, holding a wooden star that's too heavy for the top of the tree.

'The pie's ready,' Thea calls from the kitchen. 'Want some?'

'Yes, please.' She runs out to the kitchen and thanks her mother for telling the story again.

'What's that face for, Ursula?' Thea asks.

'Nothing. Well, actually something. This time

when you told the story you said Henry and Miss Anders came on a snowmobile.'

'And?' Thea says, dishing out the blueberry pie.

'I don't remember there being a snowmobile in the story before. I thought Henry came in a lorry with Miss Anders and some other people because the cabin wasn't far from a road.'

'No, I don't think so. I was there, don't forget.'

'And I thought you left your socks for the bear, not your hat,' Ursula says. 'And you never said before that you hung paper chains in the tree.'

Thea laughs and pulls Ursula into a hug. 'Stories are always a mixture of truth and make-believe, even when they are true,' she says. 'And the more they get told, more gets added, and other things get taken away. But like the bear, the story becomes a greater thing than all the little parts. Like Christmas is to us.'

Every year, at Christmas, Ursula and Thea do something different – they invite friends, or visit a neighbour with lunch. Sometimes they don't put many decorations up, sometimes they do. Because it isn't the traditions that make the magic for them, it's the togetherness.

They take their bowls and spoons and jump on the sofa, once again wrapped in warmth and the glow of the Christmas lights as the clock ticks towards midnight when Ursula will run upstairs, dive into bed and close her eyes.

Ursula takes a spoonful of pie and blows on it. A very small part of her has never been entirely one hundred per cent sure that the part of the story about how close her mother was with a bear is completely true. It's miraculous if it was.

'I love that bear as much as you, Mum, even though I never met him,' Ursula says.

No matter what they do for Christmas, Thea has told this story every year since Ursula can remember, even though details have been changed, and Ursula once again has to decide what it means to her. Ursula scrapes out the last of her pie and puts the bowl down. They wriggle on the sofa, pulling the blanket around them again, until they are so close they overlap.

'I'm excited about tomorrow,' Ursula whispers, her eyes bright and hopeful. She links her hand into her mother's.

Thea laughs. 'I may have got you an old pair of wellies, for all you know.'

'I don't mind,' Ursula says. 'Who knows where they might take me?'

And this time Ursula wonders something new about the story. Would her mother have become a writer if she *had* got a typewriter for her birthday instead of a pair of rubber boots?

ACKNOWLEDGEMENTS

Eternal thanks to Mum and Dad. They were disappointed that they couldn't get me the typewriter that I longed for as a child, but I'm sure they now know that it was realizing my heart's desire that mattered, not the typewriter. Thank you, Mum, for letting me dictate stories to you as a child while you typed them as I stood by your side, and for teaching me to type. It has served me well all my life and inspired this story.

Sincere thanks to Julia Churchill, my agent, for her dedication to my life as an author, and to Rachel Denwood, my editor, whose heart surely must live in the same street as mine. And thank you to the wonderfully vibrant team at Simon and Schuster for pouring their enthusiasm into this book. Thank you to Fiona Woodcock for bringing the bear and his landscape to life with such beautiful illustrations. Thank you to family and friends who continue to spur me on by asking what I'm writing next.